Then—then the gold iridescent glow pulled itself together, shrinking into a dark gray shadow, like thunder clouds suddenly gathering and blotting out the sun—shrinking and immediately expanding into a slowly whirling shape that grew ever larger until it filled the dish, spilling out like vapor over the fluted edges, then gathering itself again to form a face.

The face held Daria spellbound, her heart pounding and breath locked tight in her throat, so that she could not speak or even whisper. She stood staring at the face in the dish. It seemed to pulsate like a warm and living thing.

As she gazed at the face in the dish, Daria heard a soft rustle of laughter, a caressing murmur, "Love child. You, Daria. You are a love child. . . ."

BEYOND ANOTHER DOOR

Sonia Levitin

FAWCETT JUNIPER • NEW YORK

A Fawcett Juniper Book
Published by Ballantine Books
Copyright © 1977 by Sonia Levitin

All rights reserved under International and Pan-American Copyright Conventions. Published in the United States by Ballantine Books, a division of Random House, Inc., New York, and simultaneously in Canada by Random House of Canada Limited, Toronto. Originally published by Atheneum Publishers, Inc., in 1977.

Library of Congress Catalog Card Number: 76-41184

ISBN 0-449-70425-4

Till We Meet Again (Raymond B. Egan-Richard A. Whiting) © 1918 Warner Bros. Inc. Copyright Renewed. All Rights Reserved. Used by permission.

Manufactured in the United States of America

First Ballantine Books Edition: April 1994

10 9 8 7 6 5 4 3 2 1

For Shari, with lots of love
and for the gang from Malaga Cove

ACKNOWLEDGMENTS

I am grateful to the following friends
for sharing their time and their special insights with me:

Dr. Kelly Bennet
Glenn Falkenstein
Karen Rose
Jane Shuttenhelm
La Vada Weir

1

*

Sometimes when the sky was overcast, like now, Daria would get a strange longing for something she could not quite explain. She felt then that if she were to close her eyes and really concentrate, she'd arrive at some half-forgotten, long-desired destination. She would be coming home.

For a moment she closed her eyes against the swirling fog outside. Her gray, white-ruffed cat, Priscilla, stretched out a tentative paw. Daria gathered the cat up in her arms.

"Carnival time," she crooned, rubbing her chin against Priscilla's soft fur. "It's always foggy for carnival, Miss Priss. Most towns have carnivals when it's sunny. Not Marble Beach. Oh, no. We get carnival every April, when you can hardly see two feet in front of your face."

The cat only blinked. She was dignified and silent. Unlike certain neighborhood felines, she neither yowled at the toms nor picked scraps from the trash cans. If a dog approached, she'd puff up her fur and solemnly outstare him until he retreated.

"In exactly five minutes," she told the cat, "Kelly will phone to see if I'm ready to go. Want to bet?"

Solemnly Priscilla let Daria shake her paw. Daria smiled, then sighed, staring wistfully out into the fog. On a fine day she could see the distant edge of the ocean from her bedroom window. Now the horizon was lost in a gray haze.

Some view. Her mother, whenever she brought over a new acquaintance from the bank, would swing open Daria's bedroom door and announce, "I gave my daughter the *view* room. She can see the ocean from here. Would you believe it? Whoever dreamed, back in Missouri, that we'd be living at the edge of the Pacific?"

That confounded view. Her mother really had a thing about that view.

"You don't even appreciate your view!" she'd yell at Daria suddenly.

"Well maybe that's why it disappears into fog so often," Daria would shout back, "because I don't *appreciate* it!"

"Don't be so fresh. If I hadn't given you the best room . . ."

"Want to trade?"

"Of course not. I'm only saying, if you at least appreciated . . ."

Daria hated that word. Sometime she'd write it on a piece of paper a hundred times, then rip the paper into bits and burn it in an ashtray. That would make her mother yell, too.

"Daria, what in God's name are you doing in there? I smell something burning. Are you lighting matches, Daria? Are you burning incense again? I told you, incense gives me a headache."

Daria pondered their differences. Her mother often pointed them out. "I'm a practical person, Daria. And thank God one of us is. You're a dreamer. Well, I always say, behind every dreamer there's a practical person to lean on."

Lazily Daria traced the outline of a stick figure on the moist window pane. Round and round she formed the figure, giving it a hat, a tie . . .

A man. A man coming home for dinner. A man coming

home from the office for dinner, carrying a briefcase. His little girl looks up from the TV. She runs to him, puts her arms around him. He gives her a hug, and she shrieks, "Daddy! Daddy!"

With one swift, firm motion Daria wiped the window clean. Vigorously she began to brush her hair until it snapped and crackled. Then the telephone rang.

"Dari? Want to leave now? I'll meet you on the corner."

"Sure, Kelly. But I've got to be home by seven."

"Bummer."

"Yeah."

It was sort of a game they played, that complaining, because their mothers were both alike about certain things, like when to come home in the evening. Once Daria's mother had looked quizzically at the two of them and said, "Isn't this just a game? You kids always complain so automatically, almost as if it were expected of you." She had smiled, without malice.

"Oh, sure, Mom." Daria had made her voice heavy with sarcasm, while inside she'd felt a tingling of mirth. It was true. But how did her mother know?

Her mother, Peg Peterson, was as practical as a fence post, as she herself said. Seldom did she try to look beyond the obvious. She refused to let herself be drawn into what she called "no-end" discussions, and she called abstract questions "stuff and nonsense." To Daria, such "nonsense" was delicious. She and Kelly, for instance, would discuss their dreams by the hour. They could talk endlessly about questions that had no answers, where the very asking provided the thrill. Well, that was why they were friends. They'd been friends for over three years, ever since fifth grade.

Now Daria, walking toward Kelly, saw her friend start up the steep hill, legs pumping, arms swinging energetically. Kelly gave the impression of constant motion, a glittering sort of movement like quicksilver.

From the corner where the hill crested, Daria called down, "Hey! Stay there. I'm coming down to meet you."

"Yes, Mama!" Kelly called back, sticking out her tongue.

Daria, panting from the momentum of her downhill run, gasped out. "There's no point in you coming all the way up when we'd just have to walk down again anyhow."

"You don't want me to start wheezing again," Kelly said grimly.

"Oh, Kelly, I wasn't even thinking of that. Honestly. I just think it's silly to walk all the way . . ."

"OK, Dari. Forget it."

They walked easily in rhythm, although Daria's legs were many inches longer than Kelly's. Kelly, wearing Levis and a hooded blue sweatshirt, still managed to look like those girls modeling clothes in teen magazines. With her large dark eyes and curling black hair, Kelly was undoubtedly the prettiest girl in their grade. Her skin glowed smooth and tan in a look of vitality that Daria could never describe. It made her feel happy when other kids said about her best friend, "Isn't Kelly Baxter a doll? Isn't she cute?"

In looks, Daria was Kelly's opposite—blue eyes, blond straight hair, and tall. Perhaps, Daria thought, it is true that opposites attract. Even their movements were different.

Kelly, bouncing as she walked, jingled the coins in her pocket. "I've got nearly four bucks," she said. "This year, I swear, I'm going to win one of those stuffed animals. Remember the big ones from last year?"

Daria nodded. "I'd take that long green snake, wouldn't you?"

"It's a crocodile," Kelly said, quickening her steps. "That's what I'll win tonight, and I'll name it Charlie,

4

after Charlie Lacey.'' She giggled and flushed, as always when she mentioned his name.

The faint hum of music became audible—not actual music, but rather those musical sensations that signify carnival. With it came, gradually, the smell of popcorn and cotton candy, root beer and hot dogs, all wafting in on the fog, along with the bright lights of the midway and the colored lights of the Ferris wheel, now beaming through the haze.

''What are you going to try for?'' Kelly asked, nearly running but holding back, too.

''I'll try for anything,'' Daria said, laughing, ''but a fat lot of good it'll do me. I never win anything.''

''You won that art contest last year,'' Kelly reminded her.

''I mean I never win things at raffles or fairs. I'm lousy at hitting targets. I'd rather spend my money on the rides and the food.''

Kelly dashed ahead. ''Let's go to the booths!''

Daria let herself gradually be caught up in the atmosphere of the carnival. It was fun, and yet, whatever she expected, it didn't quite happen. While she let herself be swept into the motions of it all—the frantic speed of the rides, the flashing lights, the taste and smell of carnival fare, the crowds of people laughing, screaming, waving and pushing—while all this was exciting, still something seemed to be missing.

''Want to call home and see if we can stay longer?'' Kelly asked after several hours. ''Otherwise we'll have to leave in fifteen minutes.''

''OK,'' Daria replied.

''Don't you care?''

Daria shook her head. ''Maybe we're outgrowing this stuff.''

"Oh, really? You wanted to go on that Ferris wheel five times."

"That's different," Daria said, laughing.

Both together they called out, "Remember how we . . ." and they both giggled, sharing the memory of their first meeting right in front of this same Ferris wheel.

Of all the carnival trappings, only the Ferris wheel stood here in Carni Square all year round. It was a landmark in Marble Beach, left from the old days when the boardwalk featured a full-scale amusement park. The boardwalk was long since gone, replaced by high-rent apartment buildings.

Three years ago they had met right in front of the Ferris wheel, two ten-year-olds standing with their mothers, waiting for the ride. The mothers had started to talk, and then the girls rode the Ferris wheel together and a friendship began.

Now Daria said, "There's no point in calling my mom anyhow. She wouldn't let me stay any later."

"Yeah," Kelly said gloomily. "My mom's been so overprotective lately it's sickening. She just *watches* me, you know? Like sometimes I'll catch her just staring at me."

"That's 'cause you're so gorgeous," Daria quipped.

"Oh, shut up, Dari. Come on, let's do the penny toss once more."

"Kelly, I'm not throwing my money around, even if it is just a penny. It's the principle of the thing."

"You sound just like your mom," Kelly said, grinning. "When you talk like that, you even look like her."

Laughing, they walked toward the booth. A man and a teenage boy stood in the center, ready to rake in the pennies of the poor suckers who kept tossing them away. A fat woman just ahead of the girls leaned her arms on the counter where she had stacked five bank rolls of pennies. Beside her, a fat little girl stood sullen and pouting, occasionally whining, "You promised you'd win me something!"

"Pitch a penny! Pitch a penny!" the boy called out in perfect carnival barker style. "Step right up, my lovely ladies," he said grandly, touching his black bow tie and giving a bow from the waist. "Try your luck, won't you?"

He was Rob Turner, whom they'd known in a vague way since grammar school.

"Step right up, my friends!" Rob called, beaming. "Let's see what you can win for a common penny, just one cent."

Here in the glittering booth, Rob's dark eyes held a vitality that Daria had never noticed in school. He sat several seats behind her in English, but he never spoke to her and seldom joined in class discussions. Now Rob Turner seemed to have been transformed.

Daria sensed a subtle transformation in herself, too. Words tumbled out gaily, with just the right quality of teasing. She gave Rob a bright smile. "Since you've got such gorgeous wares, we'd be silly not to try. Where else can you find dishes of pure gold, and silver boxes with real jewels, all for a lowly penny?"

"Right-o!" Gleefully Rob pointed with his rake to the pasteboard boxes and dusty dishes arranged on the gaming table.

"This crystal," he said grandly, "is imported from Sweden."

"And those spoons!" Kelly exclaimed, getting into the spirit. "Wouldn't you say they're at least fourteen carat gold?"

"Definitely," Daria nodded.

"Toss a penny!" shouted Rob. "Toss a penny!" He stepped back as Kelly, leaning over as far as she dared, aimed a penny at one of the plates. The penny landed on the ground.

7

"Too bad. Lady Luck stepped out for a moment. Try again!"

Again and again Kelly tossed her pennies, until her smile faded and she complained, "This is stupid. I'm nearly broke."

Rob Turner leaned toward them across the booth. "How about you, Daria? Are you afraid to risk a penny?"

She shook her head. "Listen, I could stand here and toss two hundred pennies and I'd never win anything. You've probably got all that stuff greased or something. How come nobody wins anything?"

As if to prove her accusation, several boys tossing pennies from the other side of the booth groaned loudly as their money ricocheted off the dishes and landed on the floor. The man swept the pennies swiftly away, out of sight.

"Lots of folks have won things," Rob said, though he seemed weary now and his smile was unsteady.

"All right," Daria said. "I'll try one. Just one, to prove to you . . ."

While she spoke, she leaned forward ever so slightly, and, scarcely looking, she tossed out her penny. It landed square and solid, with a tiny ringing noise, in the center of a dish.

Immediately Rob scooped up the dish and presented it to her, calling out loudly, "Another lucky winner! Here's your prize, miss!"

A small crowd quickly gathered. Kelly and Daria moved away from the booth and away from the carnival area. For several minutes neither of them spoke. Then Kelly said softly, wonderingly, "I thought you never won anything."

"There's a first time for everything."

"You weren't even trying! You were hardly looking," Kelly said accusingly.

Suddenly angered, Daria snapped, "I can't help it I won

this crummy dish. You can have it if you want. It's just a piece of junk.''

"I don't want it," Kelly retorted. "I didn't say I wanted it. I wanted to win a stuffed animal. I spent three dollars on those dumb booths, and you only threw one penny and got a prize.''

"I can't help that.''

They walked on silently, past the small shops, beyond the business district to Beach Drive, where they would move off in different directions.

"See you tomorrow," Kelly said. Then she added, "I wonder what would have happened if you'd tried other games. Maybe it was your night—a lucky night.''

"Do you really believe in luck?" Daria asked. "Like using a rabbit's foot or stuff like astrology, where certain days are lucky?''

Kelly shrugged. "Of course not. That's just superstition. But, Dari,'' she added seriously, "I watched you tossing that penny. It was really weird. I mean, it went to that dish as if it was *attracted*, like a magnet. Didn't you see it?''

"I didn't see anything like that." Daria turned, facing up the hill. "All that happened is I won a dish. See you tomorrow.''

Strangely, her heart was pounding. As she proceeded up the steep hill, her feet began to tingle, as if they were asleep. But that was ridiculous, she thought. Feet don't go to sleep when you're walking on them. Resolutely she continued, wondering why she felt so very odd.

2

*

The seven o'clock news was on, and Daria's mother called out over the broadcaster's voice, "Have a good time?"

"Yeah. It was OK."

"Did you eat?"

"Plenty. We had dinner there. Hot dogs and stuff."

"Well, if that's how you want to spend your allowance."

Daria poured herself a glass of milk. She set it down on the kitchen table, beside the dish she had won, and sat down. The dish was about eight inches in diameter. In the bright kitchen light it seemed to glow, its colors a blending of apricot, orange and gold.

"What's that?" Her mother stopped momentarily to look at the dish.

"I won it."

"What'd it cost you to win it?"

"A penny."

"Well, I'd say you got your money's worth," Peg Peterson said briskly. She repeated, "Did you have a good time?"

"Yes. We saw lots of kids from school."

"That's nice. How's Kelly?"

"She's fine."

"No more asthma?"

"She's *fine*."

Daria stood up, took her glass to the sink and started

up the narrow half-staircase to the bedrooms. Peg called her back. "Don't forget your dish."

"I don't want it, Mom. It's for you."

"For me? Daria, really, that's sweet of you." Her mother came to the stair, holding the dish in one hand. "I really think that's sweet of you, dear, but you ought to keep it. You won it, and you could keep hairpins and things in it."

"I don't use hairpins, Mother."

"Well, whatever you want, then. It's not really a very practical size for the kitchen. I guess I could use it for fruit, but only three apples would fit into it, and it's too shallow for flowers."

"You think it's ugly, don't you," Daria said.

"I didn't say that."

"But that's what you think."

"Well, Daria, after all, it's only a carnival thing, the sort of dish you'd find in a dime store, and I don't need . . ."

Daria took the dish from her mother and turned again to go upstairs.

"Thank you, anyhow," Peg called after her. "It was sweet of you."

Upstairs in her room, Daria set the dish down on her bureau. The bureau was a low piece which doubled as a dressing table. Daria had had it since she was a baby. She knew every chip and scratch, every aberration of color. The wood had faded badly in some places. One spot was forever coated with a patch of dull pink nail polish.

Her furniture was all like that—the rocker with its cane seat half torn out, the four poster bed with its deep, old-fashioned mattress, and the unpainted orange-crate-like thing she used for odds and ends.

Every so often Daria's mother would decide that Daria needed a real desk to do her homework on. But Daria always talked her out of it. She did her homework either

11

on her bed or sitting on the floor, and sometimes standing up, hunched over the bureau.

The desk was a symbol, Daria knew, for all the things her mother thought a girl ought to have, which she, Peg Peterson, ought to provide but couldn't.

Daria stood looking half out the window into the fog while her eye also caught the dish. She felt sleepy, and it seemed that her vision encompassed many things at once, as if while she were standing by the window, she also stood above and apart, watching.

She had really wanted to give her mother the dish. Something to make Peg's lips soften into a smile. Well, it was just a piece of junk. And yet, it bordered strangely between vulgarity and beauty. Its rim, about two inches wide, was fluted like the edges of a pie. It glowed like an iridescent lipstick, apricot-orange, with a thin patina of gold.

Daria sat down on her bed, running her fingertips over the raised pattern on the cheap chenille spread. Kelly's bedspread was a beautiful bold patchwork, each patch of a brilliant hue. Kelly's drapes were a rich royal blue. Her furniture was of an elegant dull walnut, and everything matched.

From somewhere Daria heard the echo of a voice. "Envy, my dear, is one of the least attractive emotions."

Cool and lime green, the mind-voice crackled like ice crackling in lemonade on a hot summer day. The words themselves seemed to form shapes, hazy shapes whose main property was color—lime green, pale yellow, milky white.

From her bureau Daria took up the sketch pad that she always kept near. With a charcoal pencil she began to draw shapes, like large ink blots, until one of the shapes gave her the impression of personhood, and she added eyes, nostrils and a moustache.

12

"Creating, my dear?" Her mother's presence startled Daria.

"I—I was just fooling around."

"A school assignment?"

"No. Mom . . ." She hesitated, then took a chance. "Mom, do you ever think about words having—um—being in color? I mean, certain sayings, do you ever imagine them as having an actual shape?"

"Never." Peg Peterson frowned and pursed her lips. For several moments she stared at Daria. Then she laughed, a laugh that seemed to Daria to be brittle, and if it possessed a color it would have been grayish purple.

"I guess you're trying to develop what some people call an 'artistic temperament,' aren't you? Well, maybe you will use your art someday. Maybe not. Just be prepared to do something solid. Get a real skill. Somehow the women in our family always seem to end up having to support themselves and their . . ."

She stopped abruptly, murmured, "Good night," and closed the door swiftly behind her.

At school the next day Rob Turner went to sharpen his pencil before class, stopping at Daria's desk. "Did you like the carnival? Are you coming back tonight? I get a buck eighty an hour for working there all this week."

He pushed back his hair, which fell straight down again. Brown hair, light as taffy, it seemed too soft for a boy, but his eyes were intense and very dark.

He continued, as if they were old friends. "A dollar eighty isn't bad. Especially when you figure I get to eat all I want from the concessions. Are you coming back tonight? You should try the other booths. I mean, with your kind of luck . . ."

Rob lowered his voice. "I've been in that booth four

13

nights now. I never saw anything like what happened last night."

Daria said, "So I won a dish. Big deal."

"But you weren't even looking!"

The teacher, having settled herself, rapped for order.

"I don't know what you're talking about," Daria said, focusing all her attention onto her book and the teacher's dry, stern voice.

After class, when Rob smiled and said, "Will I see you at the carnival again?" Daria only shrugged and finally said stiffly, "Maybe."

Later, telling Kelly about it, she couldn't understand her own icy rudeness to Rob.

"Well, he isn't exactly a fox," said Kelly. "He isn't anything like Charlie Lacey."

"Everybody in the world doesn't happen to faint every time Charlie Lacey walks by," Daria retorted. "Rob's nice, really. I don't know why I was mean to him."

"Do you want to go to the carnival tonight, then?" Kelly asked.

Daria paused, then with a shiver she said, "No. It's too cold out, too foggy."

But it wasn't the fog. Another kind of coldness seemed to hover near her, and it had nothing to do with the weather.

"You were going to sleep over tonight," Kelly reminded her. "We can go to the show."

"OK," Daria said, without enthusiasm.

"What's wrong with you? Don't you want to do anything?"

"Sure. Go ahead and find out what's playing." It didn't matter. Even while Daria spoke, she knew, somehow, that they wouldn't be going to the movies tonight. She would not be spending the night with Kelly at all.

"What's wrong, Daria?" Kelly repeated, hands on hips.

14

"Don't you want to spend the night? If you don't, just say so."

"It's not that, Kelly." Daria sighed. "I've got a funny feeling that no matter what we plan, it won't work out."

"What are you talking about?" Kelly glanced around nervously. "Why wouldn't it work out? Are you sick?"

"No." Daria smiled to prove it. "I can't explain it. I just have this feeling."

"That's the creepiest thing I ever heard!" Kelly exclaimed.

"Look," Daria said with a shrug, "forget what I said. Let's go straight to your house, and we'll decide later about the show. Did your mom say I could stay over?"

"Sure. I asked her this morning."

Mrs. Baxter met them at the door, dressed to go out. "Hi, kids. Kelly, I'm so glad you came home in time. You can have a glass of milk before we . . ."

"We just want to go to my room, Mom," Kelly said.

"Wait a minute." Mrs. Baxter stopped them. "I hate to do this to you girls, but I'm afraid Daria can't stay over tonight. We've got to go to the valley to see your Aunt Fay. We'll be staying overnight. She's been awfully upset, ever since her mother-in-law died. Dad's driving out from the office later tonight."

"But why can't I stay at Daria's then?" Kelly argued. "I don't want to go out there!"

"You have to come with us tonight, Kelly. Please don't fuss. We haven't got time for that now. Just pack a few things and let's get going. We'll have Daria another weekend."

"Golly, Mom," Kelly cried. "You promised . . ."

As Daria went to the door, she caught Kelly's glance. In that look of Kelly's was a coldness Daria had never seen before. Kelly started, amazed and afraid, but Daria also saw a shudder of revulsion.

It would be another long, boring Friday night. Daria waited at home alone for the hour before her mother returned from work, hoping that at least her mom would take her to Luigi's for pizza. But the moment her mother walked in, she called out, "Say, Daria, would you mind fixing yourself a can of spaghetti or something?" Peg stepped out of her shoes, walking with them in her hand up the stairs to her bedroom.

Wordlessly Daria followed. It was a ritual, every movement of which had been etched into her mind since she was a baby. Only then, of course, there had been a succession of baby-sitters to tend her, usually widows who fed her too many cookies and said, "Hush, hush now," and referred to Daria as "we." "My, aren't we looking bright and chipper today! Shall we wash our hands before dinner?"

Her mother sat down on the stiff little chair, covered to match her bedspread. "One of the new women at the bank," she said, "asked me to go out to dinner and a movie. I thought I should. I mean, she's new here and probably needs . . ."

"It's OK, Mom." She hated it when her mom felt she had to justify every little pleasure, even dinner out, probably just a hamburger at Polo Joe's, and a lousy show.

"Are you sure?" Peg seemed relieved. "You can have that canned spaghetti you like, and I've got some fresh berries."

"That's fine. I don't mind staying alone."

For a moment Peg Peterson's features softened. She let her hand rest on Daria's shoulder. "I know. Thanks, Dari. You see, I . . ."

But the telephone rang. It was the new friend from the bank, and the moment vanished, incomplete. Soon Daria was alone again, having known it would be like this, exactly like this.

She went about the motions of fixing spaghetti, eating by the TV, then moving languidly up the stairs to her room, to stand gazing out into the fog, her vision taking in the window frame, the bureau with everything on it—her sketch pad, charcoal pencils, hairbrush and the dish. The dish.

Gold and apricot-orange, the dish seemed to glow as if a fire were contained in it. Its substance, its essence *was* luminousness and—life.

"Ridiculous!"

Daria spoke the word aloud, and from the corner of her eye she saw Priscilla suddenly awaken from her slumber on the bed. In one single motion, the cat drew herself into a ball. Hair stood out like quills. The cat's ruff bristled, while her tail flicked back and forth, back and forth.

From the edge of her vision Daria saw this, while her eyes still were focused upon the dish, drawn to it by a force that seemed to come from the dish itself.

Then—then the gold iridescent glow pulled itself together, shrinking into a dark gray shadow, like thunderclouds suddenly gathering and blotting out the sun—shrinking and immediately expanding into a slowly whirling shape that grew ever larger until it filled the dish, spilling out like vapor over the fluted edges, then gathering itself again to form a face.

The face appeared complete. In that instant Priscilla let out a yowl of utter anguish, and in a flying arc, leaped from the bed out into the hall.

The face held Daria spellbound, her heart pounding and breath locked tight in her throat, so that she could not speak or even whisper. She stood staring at the face in the dish. It seemed to pulsate like a warm and living thing.

As she gazed at the face in the dish, Daria heard a soft

17

rustle of laughter, a caressing murmur. "Love child. You, Daria. You are a love child."

With the words a faint and familiar fragrance bloomed about her and again came the hushed murmur. "Love child."

3

*

Sunlight crept in under the edges of her window blind, leaving diagonal stripes of light across the carpet.

Daria lay very still, gazing about the familiar room. Everything was as usual. Every small rose and bramble on the faded wallpaper was in place. The edge where the paper met was still peeling. The spot on the rug where Priscilla had had her kitten still showed.

Daria turned slightly, stretching carefully, as though she were very fragile. She could not remember having gone to bed. Somehow she had landed there, gotten under the covers and slept soundly until morning.

Now she remembered. Just before she slept, she had caught her own reflection in the mirror. Her expression had been identical to the look she had seen a few hours earlier on Kelly's face.

Slowly Daria got up and went to her bureau. She gazed down at the dish. In the morning light, the surface gleamed like a mirror or like sunshine on a lake. Carefully she picked up the dish and held it before her face. Yes, reflected there was her own image, hazy and irregular, but her own true image nevertheless.

She pulled on her jeans and ran the brush through her hair. Quickly, almost gleefully she made her bed. She certainly ought to know the kind of crazy tricks that the darkness can play on people! Wasn't she familiar enough with darkness to know better? Ever since she could remember, there had been dark rooms where she slept alone at night. She used to hear strange noises and to imagine shapes in the shadows.

Daria put on a blue and green plaid shirt, and the colors caught her complexion, giving it a deeper, more healthy, tan. Beside the vivid plaid, her hair was more purely blond, and her eyes, usually gray, took on a richer, clearer blue.

Saturday. Saturday. The precious word was like a song in her mind, in her whole being. Saturday. Day of choices and infinite variety. What to do? Kelly would be gone all day. But she could call any one of half a dozen other kids in their crowd—Claire Bennioff or Sue Hamlin, Midge Walters, Nan McGraw. She could call any one of them, and they'd go to the show or browse through the boutiques or take the bike trail all the way to Point Loma, or just sit on the sand and talk, watching the surfers and the sailboats.

Instead, without even consciously forming the thought, Daria told her mother, "I think I'll go down to the carnival this morning."

"Oh? I thought you were outgrowing it."

"Did I say that?"

"You implied it. Several times. Well, go ahead. Have a good time. Would you stop on the way home and bring me some instant coffee? Here's a coupon."

"How about money for the coffee?"

Carefully Peg Peterson counted out the exact amount. "Get the large jar. More economical."

"Mom." Daria glanced at her mother's profile. In that instant it seemed that if Peg should turn, something hidden would be known. What was it? Sometimes Daria felt almost on the verge of catching some elusive thought, something that lay just a bit further back in her memory than she was able to go.

"I guess you'll want lunch money," Peg said briskly. "Will seventy-five cents do it?"

"Sure. I'll be back by three."

"I'll be here. Chores today. My Saturday. Have to wax the kitchen floor."

Daria fled from the grim recital that would surely follow. She jogged down the hill to Beach Drive, then took up a more dignified pace. Priscilla, who had come streaking behind her, made her way slowly back to the apartment.

It was too early for carnival goers yet. Several men were hosing down the area, making the spray whisk away crushed popcorn and candy wrappers and cigarette butts. In the morning dampness Daria shivered and wished she'd brought her jacket. She folded her arms and walked with her back hunched slightly against the cold. In the gray morning, with the cold wetness underfoot, the carnival seemed the drabbest, shabbiest place in the world. Tonight the whirling colors, the mouth-watering scents and the chorus of laughter would transform junk into jewels and drab booths into fairy castles. Now it was merely dirty and a little sad, like the filthy mutt who poked his nose into the debris and ran aimlessly to and fro.

"Hey!"

She walked on.

"Daria. Daria Peterson!"

It was Rob, taking long-legged strides toward her, waving. "I didn't think you'd come out in the *morning*."

"I didn't either," she said, smiling slightly. It was a casual smile, without any of the flirtatious undercurrent of the earlier night.

He caught up with her, and without ceremony or comment took her arm. For an instant Daria felt herself pause—more a mental pause than physical. He certainly was acting possessive!

21

"Let me show you the carnival behind the scenes," he said, smiling, "the real show."

Daria laughed and quickened her steps to match Rob's. "Where are we going?"

"Don't you want to meet the carnival crowd?" He pressed her arm slightly. "Isn't that why you came?"

"I don't know exactly why I came," Daria said seriously.

"Doesn't matter. I'm glad you did."

They walked past the stalls still covered with their night canvases. The popcorn vendor was cleaning out last night's stale supply. He looked up and offered, "You kids want some popcorn?"

"Sure!" Rob, grinning, accepted a huge sackful, and they walked along, eating.

"Where is everybody?" Daria asked at last. "The carnival crowd?"

"People you wanted," Rob said with a flourish, "and people you'll get."

They had come to a booth draped in red and black, with large silver stars sewn into the fabric, and above it a large sign that said, "Madame Minerva. Fortunes Told."

Heedless of the debris, Rob sat down before the booth, cross-legged. From his back pocket he took a large white handkerchief and solemnly wound it around his head.

Daria, watching, bent over, convulsed with giggles.

"You're sitting in a puddle!" she cried, laughing. "Rob, you're absolutely the craziest . . ."

"You weel see that such terms are not to be lightly bespoken, not at all. You weel listen to theese fortune, and forget about such things as bepuddled."

Frowning deeply, turning the corners of his mouth downward, Rob held his hands cupped before him, as if holding a crystal ball, and he began to intone, "You—you are a person of rare and extraordinary geefts. These geefts

22

are as yet to be unfolded and beknown. You have thee geeft of prophecy. Madame Minerva will now predict your future, but for the small betokenment of twenty-five dollars!"

Still laughing, Daria reached into the hip pocket of her jeans. "Here, Madame Minerva," she said, holding out the coins. "I don't happen to have twenty-five dollars. Would seventeen cents do?"

"Perfectly!" Rob exclaimed, widening his eyes in avaricious delight. "Ah, now, thee crystal becomes much becleared, much better she gets when there is money in the hand. It is quite amazing.

"As I said, you are blessed with thee power of prophecy. And you are very good in school, but not too superior, eh? On your report card you weel get two or three A's, some B's, a C, and several other marks that are not too becleared."

"What's the C in?"

"Math."

"You know I'm a dud in math."

"Of course. Madame Minerva knows all theengs. Pay more dollars to Madame Minerva, and she weel tell all."

Daria dug into her pockets and came up with four more pennies.

"This is it, Madame Minerva. Tell all. I dare you."

"You weel be a great beauty."

"Oh, really?"

"Really. You are already—how you say—not an ugly duckling."

"What is this gift you're talking about, Madame Minerva?"

"It ees—um—the ability to know things before they happen. Precognition, it ees called, my dear, in psychic terms. Right now," he continued, pulling down the corners of his mouth to keep from grinning, "you doubt your

23

own powers. Right now, and thees very minute, you are able to see into tomorrow. You see that tomorrow you weel be lying on the beach with—yes—a boy about five feet six inches tall, light brown hair, brown eyes and skeeny. He ees wearing yellow bathing shorts. You see all this clearly, but you do not admit it.''

''My vast power scares me,'' Daria said, rolling her eyes.

''My power,'' said Rob, making his voice sound wavery, ''is fading. Fading. I feel it ebb. Have you any last questions to ask Madame Minerva? Any last questions. Any last . . .''

''One question. What is a love child?''

The moment Daria heard herself say the words, she was astounded. They had tumbled out. Simply tumbled out, without her plan or will.

Rob's eyebrows shot up. ''Ah, my leetle one weeshes to know such things as are very secret.''

''I was just kidding, Rob,'' Daria said, taking his arm. ''Get up. Come on. Let's see if any of the booths are opening.''

''A love child, my ignorant leetle pigeon . . .''

''Look! I think they're trying out the Ferris wheel. Let's see if they'll give us a free ride. Come on, Rob.''

But, oblivious to Daria's urging, Rob kept his expression frozen into his Madame Minerva frown and said, ''A love child, of course, is a child born out of wedlock. An illegitimate child. In common parlance, my dear, a bastard.''

4

*

She scarcely even realized she had been running—running as if her life were at stake. She ran past Rob, between the carnival booths, outside the carnival area and into the streets. She sped past the shops that were just beginning their Saturday trade, beyond Beach Drive and up the hill.

Tears blinded her. Then she was forced to stop, doubled over by the sharp pain in her side.

From the street below she heard Rob calling her name. Perplexed, shouting with his hand cupped to his mouth, he gazed up and down Beach Drive.

Daria stepped back, crouching in one of the doorways. Soon she saw him walk on and disappear. She remained there in the doorway, squatting down. There were no more tears. There was no feeling in her hands and feet. Looking down at her knees, she saw that they were trembling.

But why should she tremble? Why should she feel this ache?

Love child. Illegitimate. Born out of wedlock. Bastard.

The ugly, coarse-sounding word seemed to vibrate in her brain. Bastard. Child of lust. Accident. Mistake. A dirty word.

She knew the word. She knew all the words written in certain books or scrawled onto walls. What she did not know were some of the other words, like "love child."

Sometimes her mother, carefully seated on the sofa,

arms crossed in front of her chest, would speak to Daria in that tone of fake nonchalance.

"I don't know, Daria—uh—whether you have—um—how much sex education you get at school. Or what sort of things. You will want to know—things. Like, you are getting to the age where soon you will be getting your period. Menstruating."

"I know that, Mom."

"Maybe you want to discuss it with me. I—want you to know. Um. That I'm ready to discuss anything . . ."

"You think I don't know anything!" Daria had yelped, recoiling. "You think I'm so dumb. Listen, I'm not going to get my period for *ages*!"

It was a lie, of course. It would not be long now. She knew it. She could tell by the changes in her own body. The new, fragile feeling. The shape of herself, and the thoughts.

She and Kelly talked about it. Sometimes it seemed as if they never talked about anything else but sex. But try telling that to Peg Peterson. Try having a discussion and asking her real questions about how it feels or how one knows what to do or all those things that you wonder about.

But a bastard—everybody knew that word. The kids at school laughed about things like that. Last year one of the ninth grade girls got pregnant. Mary Hazeltine. Everybody knew who the guy was. Everybody knew when she had an abortion.

That was what girls did now. Had an abortion if they "got into trouble." But if you were smart, you just took the pill and didn't have any problems. No. Not if you were smart.

But thirteen years ago . . . didn't they have? . . .

Didn't have what, you idiot? Another voice mocked her. Daria, you ninny, do you really think they didn't have the pill thirteen years ago?

26

Then why didn't she use it? Was she stupid? Didn't she care? Oh, prim and perfect Peg Peterson—didn't she even know, at the age of twenty, how babies are made?

Impossible.

Then—why?

And the lies. All these years. "Daria, your daddy died when you were just a baby. He died in the war, honey. He was brave and good, and he's gone, but we still love him." And the diversions. "Let's bake some cupcakes and not think about sad things. Let's make a new dress for your doll."

Lies. There was no daddy. No real father. Yes, a guy, who wanted to make it with Peg Peterson, and maybe laughed about it afterward. Probably he never knew about any baby. And if he knew, didn't care. Just went off and got killed. Not even in battle, he was hit by a truck. The idiot! The clumsy idiot!

Slowly, as if she had been asleep, Daria stood up. She leaned for a moment against the wall of the building. Where could she go?

Farther up the hill she could see the edge of her own building. Inside, Peg Peterson was muttering over her Saturday chores, counting out all the sacrifices she made for her child.

Hypocrite! Daria clenched her fists at her sides. Loathing filled her, like a bitter taste in her mouth, at the thought of all the countless lectures that had been flung at her—all those sacrifices made by poor mama for Daria, Daria who never asked to be born, but who appeared *just because Peg Peterson was careless*.

She couldn't go home. Not now. She had to think.

Daria moved out from the doorway, gazing down the steep hill, past the rooftops and toward the water. Now, just rising out of the fog, she could see the slate blue ocean. Oh, to go there and walk on the beach for miles

27

and miles, let the smell and the feel of the surf wash over her. But no. Rob was down there somewhere, looking for her.

If only Kelly were home! But Kelly was out in the San Fernando Valley, roasting in the heat, working up a beautiful golden tan to wear to school on Monday, like a new blouse.

She could go to Sue Hamlin's or somebody else's house, wait it out, maybe be invited to spend the night. No. What could she possibly say to any of them?

Aimlessly she began to walk, and as she walked the rising salt sea air worked a soothing effect. Reason returning, her mind began to focus on certain questions.

Now, wait just a minute, the mind-voice commanded. *What really happened that's so terrible? All that happened is that Rob defined the words. Love child. Bastard.*

But he was talking about me!

Who said?

The voice. You know. The voice from the face in the dish.

Face in the dish. Oh, sure. Daria, think. How could there be a face in a dish? Furthermore, how could it speak? On top of that, even if it did speak, why would you accept such a thing as the truth? Why believe a kooky thing like that more than your own mother?

She walked faster and faster, head down, watching her feet. Instinctively she paused at the corners, dodged other pedestrians. The purposefulness of her steps, the set of her jaw, implied a destination. But she had none.

Think. Admit it. It was your own reflection in that dish or maybe the reflected shadows of a tree outside.

There is no tree outside my window. And how could I have made up the words "love child" when I never heard it before?

You must have heard it. Filed it away in your mind. The

28

human mind is amazing. It stores information like a computer. Besides, what makes you believe "love child" applies to you?

Because when Rob said it, it felt true. Some things feel right and true. Like when you meet somebody, and you know right away that they'll be your enemy or your friend. It fits. It makes things come together.

That's because you're always mad at your mother. That's why you're so quick to think the worst. You're unfair.

On and on, the mental dialogue repeated itself. Daria felt the heat of the day seep down through the fog layer and settle itself over everything. She pulled out her shirt-tails, tied them in a knot at her waist. Still she found no relief from the sultry heat as she walked on and on.

After a time she became aware of a rhythmic, harsh sound, and realized it was her own heavy breathing. She was panting. Her shirt clung to her. She could feel sweat on her legs. She wiped her forehead, stared at the wetness on her hand. Motionless, she stood leaning against the nearest building.

Daria closed her eyes. The rough stucco felt cool and somehow reassuring against her cheek. When she opened her eyes, the street seemed to rise up, like ocean swells, pulsating and giving off its own heat. The heat struck Daria full in the face, nearly causing her to fall.

She tried to take a deep, deep breath. All that came were hot, shallow breaths. Again she shut her eyes.

"Daria! Are you all right? What are you doing way over here?"

Daria looked up. Before her stood Nan McGraw and Nan's mother. Both were carrying armsful of books, and Daria realized that this building was the public library. She had walked, then, for seven miles.

Daria smiled a weak, crooked smile. "So that's what

29

you do! Go to the library on Saturday. No wonder you get straight A's.''

Mrs. McGraw stepped closer. ''Dear, are you all right? You seem . . .''

''I'm OK, Mrs. McGraw. I just took a walk and . . .''

Something hot and wet seemed to seep up through the sidewalk. Concrete buckled around her. The next thing Daria knew she was in Mrs. McGraw's car. Silence surrounded her. Then Mrs. McGraw was saying, ''Nan, I'm going to go up and get her mother. She can help us get her up the stairs. Daria, just relax, dear. Lie back. You don't have to move.''

For no reason at all, Daria found herself crying. She felt no sorrow. Tears just came of themselves, sliding down her cheeks on and on and on for no reason. No reason.

She slept. While she slept, she did not dream, but thoughts and words continued to beat their way through her head. Words and thoughts whirled like racing demons, trying to get out through her skull, imprisoned there.

As from a great distance, she saw her mother at the doorway.

''Take some aspirin. The doctor said. To get that fever down. I'll rub your back with alcohol.''

''No! Please, it's freezing.''

''I have to, Daria. Your fever's 105°. We can't let it go higher. And you've got to drink something.''

''I can't sit up.''

''Just tilt your head, Daria. I've got a straw here. I'll hold the glass. Just sip a little, my baby.''

The last words, ''my baby,'' were muffled and nearly lost as once again the fog rose around Daria's head, and she slept.

In the night she awakened and knew it was very late. It must have been three or four in the morning. She could always tell by how the silence felt, how the few isolated sounds reverberated.

She turned her head, moved her arms, realized that her fever had dropped sharply. For a moment Daria just lay there, breathing deeply. She was getting better. Those awful words had stopped beating inside her head.

A small night-light glowed from over her bureau, touching everything with a mellow light. Her mother was sleeping in the rocking chair, half-covered with an old blanket. Peg's face fell to one side, and her mouth was slack. She looked defeated, slumped there asleep in the rocker. All the firmness was gone from her features, and her hair hung limp.

Suddenly Daria felt a great joy. Of course! She had the flu. She was *very sick*. Why, she'd never had such a high fever in her life. So, she'd probably already been sick on Friday night when she had seen that supposed face in the dish. Probably she'd had a flash of fever even then and had been hallucinating. With a high fever, hallucinations were possible. She knew that from her biology class. Oh, Lord, Rob Turner must think she was an idiot.

But the words, "love child." How to explain that?

Simple. Probably those words were in some popular song. She was always listening to the radio. Certainly, the words "love child," must have been part of some popular lyrics, and she had heard them without realizing it. The words had seeped into her subconscious, only to emerge when she was off guard, hallucinating. And she'd gone and made a big deal out of nothing.

Oh, Lord! Rob Turner would probably never even look at her again. Or worse, he'd tease her, call her "love child," maybe even tell people what a nut she was. Daria groaned.

Immediately her mother was awake.

"What's wrong, Daria? How are you feeling?"

"I—the fever's down, I think." She felt her mother's cool hand on her forehead.

"Yes, yes, you're right. You're in no danger now. I'll go back to my room. But I'll leave both our doors open. Call me if you need me. Be sure and call me."

Quickly Peg Peterson bent down, and Daria felt her mother's lips brushing her forehead. For an instant Daria had the great longing to be a little child again and to say, "I love you, Mom." But she only turned her face to one side, as if she were very tired.

On Sunday afternoon Rob Turner appeared at her house. The wonder of it was not that he discovered where she lived. That was easy. The real wonder was that Peg Peterson, with her dozens of rules and restrictions, allowed him into Daria's room.

First she checked. "Daria, one of your school friends is here. Rob Turner. He said he saw you yesterday and you seemed ill. Shall I send him up?"

"Sure."

"Put on your robe first."

"Mom! I'm in bed, under the covers."

Firmly Peg stood in the doorway. "Your robe, or else he doesn't come up. And," she added, "the door stays open."

"Oh, *Mother*!"

Daria jumped up out of bed, pulled on her robe and grabbed her hairbrush. Quickly she brushed her hair. A moment later Rob thrust his face inside the doorway, holding his body back behind the wall. " 'Lo! Ready for company? If not, I'll keep part of myself outside."

She laughed. "Come on in."

He did not glance around the room or stand there awkwardly. As if he were a cousin or a brother, Rob Turner strode quickly and casually to the beat-up rocking chair and sat down.

"I'm sorry you're sick. See, Madame Minerva was wrong. She saw you at the beach today with me."

Daria only looked at him, wanting to forget "Madame Minerva."

"When you ran away like that, I tried to find you. That sickness," Rob said, "certainly came on you suddenly."

She had the distinct feeling that he knew better, for he kept looking at her, as if waiting for her to explain.

"That's how it happens sometimes," she said, toying with her hairbrush. "Actually, I was feeling sick already on Friday night, but I thought I was better."

"I see." Rob stood up and walked toward the bureau. He stared down at the dish, then picked it up. "Carnival," he mused. "We sure had a busy time last night." He turned the dish over and read the inscription. " 'Hochstein Ovenware. Heatproof. Unbreakable.' I guess you'll have this forever."

"I guess so." Daria's voice sounded more serious than she had intended, for suddenly that strangely familiar fragrance was in the room again, seeming to emanate from the dish. She had not recognized the scent before. Now she realized it was "Dew Delight," the perfume she had given Peg for her birthday last February.

She remembered now, with an overwhelming clarity, how Peg had given a little gasp, and as her face went pale, two reddish spots had shown on her throat. She had smiled then, trying desperately to recover, and with a husky chuckle had explained, "I was just a bit startled, Daria. This is the perfume my mother always used to wear."

"Try it," Daria had begged. "Don't you just love the smell? Put some on."

"Later, Daria. I'll save it," her mother said, already

turning to some small chore, "and I'll keep it for a special occasion."

That "special occasion" had not yet arrived. As far as Daria knew, her mother still had not opened the perfume.

"On Sunday?" Rob was speaking, but Daria had been lost in her own thoughts. "Hey, you haven't heard a word I said."

He set down the dish, and the fragrance was no more.

"I said, would you like to go to the beach with me next Sunday? We mustn't make a liar out of Madame Minerva, you know."

"Sure, sure," Daria said. "Listen, I—I'm feeling kind of tired now."

Immediately Rob nodded and said, "Well, I've got to go. Shouldn't stay too long. Next Sunday, OK?"

When he was gone, Daria ran lightly on tiptoes into her mother's room. In her closet on the top shelf, along with several brand-new hand towels and two immaculate shoe boxes, stood the bottle of perfume, "Dew Delight," still in its box and tightly sealed.

5

*

"No, you *cannot* stay overnight at Kelly's this Saturday, Daria, and I don't want to discuss it further."

"Oh, Mom! We've been planning it for over a week."

"You always stay up too late when you sleep at the Baxters'. You've just been sick."

"That was nearly a week ago! You never let me do anything. I wish you wouldn't be so overprotective." But even Daria could tell that her tone lacked conviction. She hadn't gone back to school until Wednesday, and then she'd felt weak and fatigued.

"We'll go to bed early, then," Daria said.

"Very well. In bed by ten-thirty, and Kelly sleeps here." Peg Peterson slammed the cupboard shut in an air of finality.

"Oh, Mom . . ."

"That's it, Daria. And I want you to do some ironing. There's a great stack . . ."

"Right now? Do I have to iron now? I want to call Kelly."

"First the ironing. Then you can call."

With a deep sigh, Daria set up the ironing board and began on the clothes and pillow cases. Actually, she didn't mind ironing. She enjoyed the smell of fresh laundry, and the smooth gliding motions of the iron helped her to think.

Her thoughts these last few days had circled and eddied like a whirlpool, always returning to that unfathomable source—the dish. From the dish had come a sound, or at least the suggestion of sound. With the sound had come shadows, then a face, and with the face a fragrance—not just any fragrance, but Dew Delight.

In back of her mind Daria had felt sure her mother was using the perfume, and that the scent had been lingering in the air to waft into Daria's room. Yes, a fragrance could be so strong and sweet as to spark the imagination. She had read somewhere that the sense of smell, more than any of the other senses, has the power to kindle memory.

But she had to acknowledge that the bottle of Dew Delight was still sealed. She had to admit, despite her growing horror, that something was happening, and it was unnatural.

When she allowed her thoughts to focus on it, Daria trembled, caught between horror and an overpowering curiosity. More even than curiosity—she felt nearly obsessed, returning again and again to the dish, to pick it up and examine it, wishing for the face, at the same time dreading that specter and its dry, rustling voice. Could it be—could it possibly be a special trick dish, a magician's dish? No, she knew full well it wasn't. It was just a dish, a gaudy dime store dish with no special properties and no magic.

Then what? What was happening? Caught once again in confusion, Daria tried to extricate herself, to find some rational explanation. She began to hum, willing her thoughts back into control. Too late, that ultimate thought appeared, taunting her: it was not the dish that was to blame, but something in *her* that caused these happenings. Something unnatural *in her*! She took a deep breath, humming still, steadying her nerves. It was like a painting. A painting is only canvas and colors, given a special meaning not because of the materials, but because of something in the artist.

But a painting was something you decided to do, while this . . .

"Daria!" Her mother's voice was sharp and scolding, catching Daria completely unaware, so that the iron grazed her finger.

"What's the matter? You made me burn myself. Why do you? . . ."

"What's that song you were singing?" Peg demanded.

"What song? I wasn't singing. Can't a person even . . ."

Daria fell silent as she saw her mother clutching the kitchen chair. She eased herself into it, the way old women do.

"What's wrong, Mom?" Daria left her ironing. "Are you sick? Do you want some water?"

"No." Peg Peterson waved her aside. "It's just—I'm all right. It was that song. I didn't realize you knew it."

"Was I singing?" Daria was truly surprised.

"Humming, rather. Weren't you aware of it?"

"Well, I guess I was humming," Daria said. "But what about it? What *was* the song?"

Peg Peterson looked down at her hands. They were strong hands, freckled, with long fingers skilled at many things. Now they trembled slightly. Her eyes were closed for a moment, and she sighed.

"It was a song your father used to sing. We'd go rowing on the lake in Silveridge Park. He'd always sing that song, even before he knew he was going into the army."

"But what's the army got to do with it?" Daria sat down opposite her mother. Suddenly Peg looked young and, somehow, delicate. Her hair was soft and barely curling up at the edges, nearly the same color as Daria's, but slightly more brown than blond. Her eyes were gentle now, a hazy gray blue. Her skin was pale, nearly translucent at the throat and temples. How odd, Daria thought, to feel

37

like this, as if she were the mother and Peg the child, needing protection.

"That song," Peg said softly, "is an old World War I song. I guess your dad learned it from his father. He loved the melody. It's a sad song, you know."

Daria whispered, afraid to break the spell. "Sing it to me. Please, Mom."

"I—I'm not sure I know all the words. He'd sing while he was rowing. I remember, one evening at dusk—I always sat facing him in the rowboat . . . he said he wanted to see me. That would be his reward, he said, for all that strenuous work." She smiled, looking down at her hands. "We were there at Silveridge Park the night he told me he had to go. He sang that song then."

Peg Peterson closed her eyes again, tilted back her head slightly and sang very softly, her voice breaking on the high notes:

> *"Smile the while*
> *You kiss me sad adieu,*
> *When the clouds roll by*
> *I'll come to you.*
> *Then the sky will seem more blue*
> *Down in lover's lane, my dearie.*
> *Wedding bells will ring so merrily . . ."*

Peg's voice ceased suddenly, and she stood up, her features taut. "I never was much good at singing," she said, "and I think you must have inherited my disability."

With quick jerking movements she went to the cupboard and brought out the dishes for their supper. She worked without speaking, wiping up crumbs from the floor, washing down a cupboard that didn't even seem dirty. Then crossly she said, "Why on earth are they bringing back those old songs? Seems to me folks would like to hear something new for a change.''

Daria said nothing. She had listened closely while her mother was singing. She knew it was the tune she had been humming earlier. But she also knew, without a shadow of a doubt, that she had never, never heard that song before.

It was Friday night. Her mother was sound asleep. They'd gone to Polo Joe's for hamburgers, then home to watch TV. They had sat at the kitchen table, and for the first time in nearly a year they'd played gin rummy, each doing it for the other, to bring back something that had once been fun. It hadn't quite worked.

By ten Peg was yawning. ''I've had a hard week, Daria. You being sick and all. I was worried. I guess I'll go to bed. How about it?''

''OK. There's nothing good on TV anyhow.''

''Is Kelly spending the night tomorrow?''

''Yeah. Maybe we'll go to the show.''

''Actually, I'd rather you stayed home. I don't like you girls coming into an empty house at night, and I'll be out.''

''Out? You never said . . .''

''Just a meeting of that Secretarial Association. The notice was delayed in the mail. I like to go to those meetings. It's not good for me to stay in all the time. People need a certain—''

''All *right*, Mom! You always sound as if I don't want you to have fun. I do want you to have fun. I—''

''OK, Daria.'' Peg's voice was heavy and resigned.

They heard each other's movements through the thin walls. Daria heard her mother's radio go on. She always slept with the radio on, just faintly, until sometime in the middle of the night, only half waking, she snapped it off.

Daria, brushing her hair over and over, sighed heavily. She wished her mother would get married again. She really did. Or even that she'd date. Maybe then she wouldn't be so uptight all the time. She knew lots of kids whose mothers were divorced or widowed. Nearly all of them dated, or had a boyfriend.

Daria turned out her light, trying to sleep. Behind her closed eyelids colors appeared, flashing, advancing, receding. It was a little game she'd played with herself ever since she could remember. The colors soothed her, almost as if they were real beings with warm bodies and sweet voices.

Suddenly she was wide awake, as words filtered in between the colors. She sat bolt upright, asking herself with a start, "How did I know that song?"

Now the words of the song hung suspended in her mind, learned and remembered as if they had been drummed into her head from birth.

> *"Smile the while*
> *You kiss me sad adieu,*
> *When the clouds roll by*
> *I'll come to you . . ."*

She remembered every word, she was sure. Excited, she got out of bed. What to do?

She opened her door, tiptoed out into the hall where Priscilla's basket stood in a corner near the stair. She took up the cat and held her close. Mom didn't like her to sleep with the cat. But she knew that Daria did it, and chose not to make an issue of it.

What to do? What to do with this strange, sudden surge of energy? Maybe she'd slept too much all week. That must be it. She'd gotten so much rest that now she felt as if she could run two miles, lift herself over the high bar at the gym, or swim out to the buoys and back. She felt charged with some source of energy, like a light, that seemed to filter through her skin, collecting inside her body, spreading outward again.

Priscilla lay down against Daria's leg, rubbing herself. Then the cat jumped up into Daria's lap. She lay there, a soft ball of fluff, while Daria stroked her. But in the next instant the cat stiffened, her hair bristled, and she arched herself as for attack.

"Oh, go on," Daria whispered, standing up to let Priscilla slide off her lap. She stood at the window where she could look out at the swirling fog and at the same time look down, down into the dish.

"Love child." The merest whisper, the softest rustling of sound. "You are a love child." With it came the heavy, sweet scent of perfume, as if someone had filled the room with it.

The voice was soft and warm, in shades of pink and palest orange. "That was his song, you know. He taught it to you. Believe it."

Daria clutched at her throat. In that moment Priscilla began to claw madly at the door.

Swiftly Daria picked up the dish and stared down into it. Shadows had settled there, but they lay motionless. The voice now was silent. She saw only her own reflection, given in hazy, inaccurate fragments.

The cat was suddenly quiet. Daria patted the bed, and Priscilla leaped up.

"You and I," Daria whispered softly to the cat, "have got to watch out for our imagination. There was no face in that dish. Do you understand? I was just tense. You picked up my vibes. Cats are very sensitive to tension. Did you know that?"

Priscilla turned over on her back, docile and purring,

41

as if to compensate for her hysterical clawing of a minute before.

"So, when I get tense and scared," Daria continued, "naturally you react. There was nothing in that dish. Just my own shadow. As for the song—I know it was his song. Mom told me so. She probably sang that tune when I was small, but she forgot. Probably I did hear it recently on the radio, which made me recall it. When something gets into your *mind*, it stays there forever. As for the words, they're simple to learn, and I heard them just last night. There's nothing strange here at all, Miss Priss, no reason to panic."

The cat seemed to agree. With another faint purr she drifted off to sleep.

It was like dozens of other Saturday nights that Kelly and Daria had spent together. They went down to Polo Joe's for an early supper of hamburgers and fries, then walked back to the apartment. They talked and laughed, laid on the floor and phoned all their friends; they played some of the old games, giggling and inventing crazy new rules; they talked in their own brand of code talk, inserting a "J" before the vowel in each syllable. They washed their hair and tried on three different shades of lip gloss, and at last they spread out their sleeping bags on the rug in the usual arrangement, since they had long ago stopped arguing about who ought to use the bed.

"Is Priss sleeping with us?" Kelly settled herself down into her sleeping bag.

"Sure," Daria said, "if the fur won't bother you."

"It doesn't," Kelly said, and they both knew it was a lie. The cat hair did make Kelly sneeze, but she loved Priscilla.

"Want to keep the night-light on?" Kelly asked.

"Sure, if you do."

Daria snapped off the overhead light, leaving the night-light plugged into the wall near the bureau. They lay quietly for a while. Then softly Daria asked, "Kelly, have you ever heard of the words, 'love child'?"

"Nope."

"Have you any idea what it means?"

"No. What is it?"

"Oh, I'm not sure myself," Daria said. After another silence she said, "Well, actually, I do know. Rob told me. It's another name for—an old-fashioned way of defining a—an illegitimate child."

"You mean you and Rob talk about things like that? Good grief, if I ever went out with Charlie Lacey, I wouldn't . . ."

"It wasn't really like we talked about it," Daria began. The pounding inside her was like a barrier between them. She wanted to tell Kelly the entire episode, that bit about Madame Minerva, and the face in the dish. Tentatively she began on a new approach.

"You know, they're bringing back a lot of old songs. My mom says some of them are the same ones she remembers when she was a kid. Last night I just started humming . . ."

Daria lay very still. She ought to stop this discussion now, she thought. Stop. Why had she brought it up?

"What song?" Kelly asked, and after a silence she prodded, "What song?"

Almost in spite of herself Daria began to hum. The tune demanded words, so she sang very softly,

> *"Smile the while*
> *You kiss me sad adieu,*
> *When the clouds roll by*
> *I'll come to you.*
> *Then the sky will seem more blue*

43

Down in lover's lane, my dearie,
Wedding bells will ring so merrily
Every tear will be a memory,
So wait and pray each night for me
Till we meet again.''

The last note seemed to linger in the air, a presence between them. Suddenly Priscilla leaped straight up, yowling as if she had been smitten with a hot poker. She slammed her body against the door, while Kelly ran to turn on the light and Daria, horrified, hurled herself aside from the flashing object that flew off the bureau and struck the floor exactly where a moment earlier her head had been.

"What is it? What is it?'' Kelly shrieked. The cat scratched wildly, and Kelly screamed, "What's that smell? Do you smell it?'' Daria, her heart thumping as if it would burst through her body, stared down at the dish that lay beside her on the floor.

The dish glistened, pulsating and throbbing with an urgent life force. Kelly, her face pasty white, moved nearer to Daria, clutching her arm. She, too, stared in rigid terror at the dish.

Within the dish the shadows darkened from gray to black, gathering into themselves. The shadows swelled outward over the rim, like vapors escaping, seeping over onto the floor, and within it a voice clearly called, "Daria!''

The voice filled the dish, wafted upward until it filled the room with a strange power, so that it seemed borne on every particle of dust in the air. "Why won't you believe? That was his song. You are a love child. Daria. Accept this and now search beyond . . .''

In a voice that was alien and terrible, Daria demanded

44

of Kelly, "Do you see it? Kelly! Tell me! Do you see it, too? Do you hear it? Kelly—am I crazy, or do you? . . ."

But Kelly, stiff and speechless, only shook her head. Suddenly the breath was closed off in Kelly's throat. A slight wheezing gave way to a heavy, labored gasping, until Kelly's lips and cheeks were swollen with the effort.

Daria flung open the window and pulled Kelly toward it, taking great gulps of air, as if to give them to the congested lungs of her friend. "Kelly!" she cried. "Kelly!"

But Kelly's head rolled to one side, and her eyes were like those of an animal cruelly trapped.

6

*

It was only after Daria had telephoned Kelly's mother, and Mrs. Baxter had rushed over with the medicine, that Daria even began to collect her thoughts. Something important had to be considered, but for the moment it eluded her.

"Your breathing seems more regular now," Mrs. Baxter was saying, holding Kelly's wrist. "Are you feeling better?"

Kelly kept her eyes downcast. "I'm OK. I guess I shouldn't have let Daria call you." She paused. It seemed that all her energy was directed toward the task of breathing.

"Of course you should!" Mrs. Baxter exclaimed. "From now on, you'd better take your inhaler along when you go out. But I didn't think . . . you've had these attacks so seldom. Did you girls do any strenuous exercises?"

"No. We just walked to Polo Joe's and back."

"And the pollens aren't particularly heavy here by the beach," Mrs. Baxter mused. She looked at Kelly anxiously. "What do you think could have triggered it?"

Without even moving her eyes, Daria felt herself begging Kelly silently not to tell. Not yet. Too much was still unexplained. Too much was at stake. And then there was this elusive thing she must consider . . .

Kelly hesitated. "I suppose," she said guardedly, "it was the cat. I told Daria to let her in," she added quickly. "It was my fault."

46

"You should never sleep with a cat in the room," Mrs. Baxter said reproachfully. "I'm just glad I was home."

Beneath Mrs. Baxter's voice, Daria's thoughts focused on that elusive thing, and then she knew. It was the song. She had sung the *whole song*!

"Kelly, I'll take you home," Mrs. Baxter was saying. "Daria doesn't look too well, either. You're deathly pale, child. Maybe you're not quite over the flu yet."

She had sung all the words, not just the words her mother had sung to her the other night. She had known three other lines, to the ending, "till we meet again."

As Mrs. Baxter spoke, she was gathering up Kelly's things. "Perhaps you girls can spend the night together next weekend."

Daria stood back, waiting. Kelly would protest. Surely, Kelly would object to being dragged out in the middle of the night like a baby, when she really felt all right now. She'd tell her mother she was feeling fine and wanted to stay.

But with a half-apologetic glance at Daria, Kelly turned to her mother and said submissively, "OK, Mom. I guess you are right."

Daria stood silent, all the while wanting to clutch at Kelly's arm and to cry out, "Kelly! Don't leave now. We've got to talk about this. Kelly, I sang a song I'd never heard before. I saw a face and heard a voice. Help me! What's happening to me? Kelly, please—don't leave me."

But she only watched Kelly leaving, murmured a faint good-bye, and went to sit on her bed.

She stared down at the chaos of her room. Sleeping bags and twisted blankets, games, hairbrushes, clothes, all strewn around. Her mom would scream at her, "Clean up this mess! It looks like a pigpen in here."

Yes, it was a mess, just like her life. She herself was a

mess. Because people—sane people—did not see things in dishes.

Daria's hands felt icy cold. The cold spread through her entire body in a feeling that was not pain, but rather an agony of emptiness and terror. It could only be that she was insane. Yes, it did happen to kids. She knew where they kept kids like that. They called them "disturbed." What they really meant was crazy.

They kept them in a hospital, locked up. She knew. Once she'd had a friend whose mother had a maid, and the maid's nephew had tried to set himself on fire and was sent to a hospital. The maid used to send him things, old toys and clothes. He was all right, the maid said, but of course, there were bars on the windows, and the kids were never allowed out alone. They were kept on tranquilizing drugs.

If people do weird, crazy things, they get sent away. If she told her mother, naturally Peg would take her to the doctor. The doctor would prescribe something, and Daria would be drugged into forgetting what she had seen, until she no longer knew what was real and what was fantasy. They would say she was obviously ill. If she still insisted upon describing her visions, they would send her away. Because sane people did not see faces in dishes. They did not hear voices or know songs they'd never learned or scare their friends half to death . . .

Friends! Kelly had seen it too. Then surely it was true and real. A different and strange reality, but a *reality* that she and Kelly had shared.

Kelly had seen the face and heard the voice. She had seen the dish flying across the room. She had even commented on the fragrance. Of course, Kelly had experienced it all, and the proof lay in the asthma attack, brought on by sheer terror.

Tomorrow she would discuss it all with Kelly. Now she

regretted not having told Kelly everything from the beginning—winning the dish, the first vision—everything. Somehow, Kelly would help her, as they had been helping each other for years.

Daria lay down on her bed and turned out the nightlight. She was not afraid of the dark. Evil did not necessarily come in darkness. Evil—was it evil?

She pondered, relaxing a little, and she realized that her neck and back ached. Tension and fear had knotted her muscles, and now she ached all over.

That song. How could she have known those last lines? It was one thing to relearn words that she had known long ago and heard again the other night. But her mother had stopped at the line about wedding bells. Daria was positive of it. Then how, how could she have known those last lines?

Again Daria's muscles began to tighten.

"Relax," she told herself. "Don't panic." She made an effort to breath slowly, rhythmically.

Daria lay very still, trying to relax her feet, legs, abdomen, just as Miss Evans, the gym teacher, had them do at the end of each PE class. "Let go. Free your minds. Relax."

Daria felt her body responding. She allowed the specks and patches of color to appear behind her closed eyelids. Slowly, slowly, they took shape, and the fluttering shapes became defined. They were angels.

> *"Guardian angels round your bed,*
> *Lay ye down your sleepy head . . ."*

Ah, yes, long ago someone had whispered to her of angels. Someone had sung to her while she lay in her little bed, and the voice was dear and beautiful. How was it possible to remember back so far, so very far?

49

"Aye, the guardian angels gather round your bed, my babe, watching over you in the night. Two round your pillow, one by your hand, two at your feet, one looking down from above. But do not open your eyes, my babe, or they will disappear."

Yes, Grandma. Grandma. But how was it possible to remember?

Without sorrow or effort, Daria wept. Warm, soothing tears, they seemed to bathe some deep and long-forgotten hurt. What was it? The edge of a memory seemed to flicker for a moment before her consciousness. Then it was gone. With a deep sigh, Daria slept.

The weather forecast had promised sunshine at the beach by noon on Sunday. Rob telephoned promptly at ten.

"I'll pick you up in an hour," he said eagerly. "I'll pack a lunch. You'll see, I'm a better picnic packer than fortune teller."

"Rob . . ." Daria hesitated. "I've got to go talk to Kelly this morning. She was sick last night."

"Can't you call her on the phone?"

"No! I've got to see her in person."

"Then, when should I meet you?"

"I don't know how long it will take."

"I see." Rob's tone was flat, withdrawn. Obviously he thought she was trying to break their date.

"This is terribly important, Rob! I'm really sorry, but Kelly had an asthma attack last night, and I've just got to see her."

"That's OK, Daria," Rob said. "Why don't you just come down to the beach whenever you can. I'll be waiting for you on the sand in front of Twinkie's."

"Thanks, Rob."

"Daria! I really want to see you today."

"Yes," she said softly. "Me too."

Hurriedly Daria got herself a glass of milk and a slice of bread and made sure the kitchen door was closed. On Sunday mornings Peg slept late. Usually Daria would just leave a note and go to Kelly's or down to the pier. Sometimes she'd buy breakfast from one of the stands at the beach. It was great to get out early. But now, more than anything else, she wanted to talk to Kelly. They would discuss everything about last night and somehow, between the two of them, everything would come clear.

Mrs. Baxter answered the telephone. "Oh, Daria? Well, dear, I think Kelly's still asleep. And we're going . . ." There was a pause, and then tension in Mrs. Baxter's voice as she said almost grudgingly, "Here she is, Daria."

Kelly, too, sounded different, even in that one word, "Hi!"

"Kelly, I've got to talk to you. Can I come over?" Daria finished the last bite of her bread, in her mind already racing toward Kelly's. They'd talk for an hour or so. Then she'd go meet Rob. They'd talk more tonight, maybe Kelly could come over for dinner and spend the evening . . .

"Well, see, we're going out," Kelly said, still in that stilted tone. "That is, my folks want me to go to Pomona with them today."

"Kelly, I've got to talk to you," Daria said urgently. "About last night. *You* know. Is it that you can't talk right now? Because your mother's in the room? I can understand that you might want to keep quiet about . . ."

"Daria, I was sick last night." The words sounded rehearsed.

"I know that! But what caused it? Listen, Kelly," Daria said rapidly, "I'd never heard all the words of that song before. I just *knew* them. And the dish. Kelly, dishes don't just go sailing in midair. You heard the voice, didn't you?

It said 'love child,' and that's what I was trying to tell you, how after the carnival I started seeing this face . . .''

"I remember you asked me what a love child was," Kelly said, sounding nervous. "Then the dish fell off the bureau . . .''

"But it didn't just fall off!" Daria paused. Then she asked suddenly, "Kelly, did you tell your mother about what happened?"

Again, silence, and then Kelly's voice, sounding too high-pitched, "Yes, I did. I told her. My mother explained it all to me."

"But how could she explain it?" Daria cried. "She wasn't there! Don't you trust your own eyes and ears? Don't you trust *me*?"

Easy—Daria tried to steady herself. Screaming at Kelly wouldn't help. It would only make her more stubborn, and eventually Kelly would get mad. They'd had fights before.

Daria heard a strange, distant sound; she did not immediately recognize it. She forced herself to speak slowly, lowering her voice to a whisper. "Kelly, think back. Do you remember, I was just singing that song. I've been thinking about this—I'm sure it was the song that triggered it."

"I don't know what you're talking about," Kelly said coldly.

Bitch! Daria wanted to scream, but she held back. "Listen, Kelly, can't I come over for just a few minutes? I'll run. I can be there in less than ten minutes."

There was silence, the strained, long silence that indicated gestures were being exchanged, Kelly asking the question, her mother's firm gestures replying, *No!*

"No, Dari, really, we're leaving in just a few minutes. I'll see you at school tomorrow."

"I've got to talk to you alone," Daria said in a low voice, her palms sweating from the effort of holding back.

52

"Are you alone now, at least? Is your mother in the room?"

Another pause, then Kelly said, "I'm alone." Still there was that coldness in her voice, and fear.

Daria clutched the receiver tightly. "Don't you understand, Kelly? This is probably the most important thing that could ever happen to me—to us. You've got to help me, Kelly. I never heard that song before, I swear it. And that face in the dish—it told me things about myself. It called me by name. You heard it and saw it. I know you did! You smelled the perfume, too."

"I think you are making a lot over it," Kelly said, and between the words Daria could hear a faint wheeze. She could visualize Kelly's face growing flushed with the first effort to regain her breath. "People imagine all sorts of things in the dark. What probably happened is that Priscilla knocked the dish off the bureau . . ."

"But why would she? Didn't you see the way that thing came flying at my head? It didn't just fall *down*!"

"That cat probably heard a noise outside . . ." The wheeze became a squeaking sound, like the air being squeezed out of a balloon.

"Priscilla never howls like that," Daria argued. "You know she doesn't."

"Cats yowl like that a lot!" Kelly cried. "Especially if they're in heat."

"Kelly, you know darn well Priscilla's been spayed!"

Louder now came the whistling sound as Kelly labored for breath. "It could have been an earthquake," she gasped. "It made the dish fall. Lots of earthquakes lately . . ."

"What about the smell then?" Daria, unable to contain herself, was nearly screaming. "You mentioned it yourself. I keep trying to tell you, it's all related, the smell, the face, the voice. Kelly, you saw it, too. Why do you lie to me? You're the only person I can trust. You're my best friend, and . . ."

"Daria, we let our imaginations run away with us." She coughed, a muffled sound.

"Who said that?" Daria's tone was harsh. "Your mother?"

"We were alone," Kelly persisted, gasping, "and it was a windy night . . ." Over and over, Kelly gave the words that must have been drummed into her. But her voice began to falter amid the hacking, wheezing cough, until in a faint whisper she said, "Daria, I just can't . . ."

Kelly's voice broke as her throat tightened. She would begin to tremble and sweat in fear of choking. Daria had witnessed it twice before, that awful fear of having one's breath closed off. It must be, she thought, like being buried alive.

"Kelly!" It was a desperate cry, her own need mingled with the desire to make Kelly better, to give her space and air to breathe. "Listen, Kelly, take it easy." How could she hurt Kelly? In a rush, she recalled all the years of their friendship. She could picture Kelly, healthy, with smooth skin and sparkling eyes, and that happy bounce in her step.

"Kelly." Daria spoke softly, eagerly, her eyes wide at the realization of what she was about to do. "Now, just relax. You're probably right. We probably did have an earthquake. And earthquakes scare that cat silly."

"When the dish fell," Kelly added, still struggling, "it made Priscilla howl."

"Yes, yes. When the dish fell, it scared Priscilla, and then she scratched at the door . . ." Daria's mind raced over possible explanations to use in this game, this most earnest game. Could a person die from asthma? She didn't know. But it had been bad enough to witness Kelly's attack.

Her breathing still labored, but more calmly now, Kelly

54

repeated, "Cats get spooked in the wind." With nobody to contradict her, she might soon come to believe it.

"Yes, Kelly," Daria said softly. "I'll see you at school tomorrow."

"OK. I—I'm sorry about today. I'm really going out with my folks."

"You can still sleep over next weekend."

"I—I don't know yet. My mom said something about taking me to Palm Springs. I'm not sure."

Dully Daria repeated, "I'll see you at school tomorrow."

She hung up the telephone. She stood in the kitchen, looking around the familiar room, and suddenly she began to shiver uncontrollably.

If she was not crazy, then someone—or something—had moved in upon her, to change her whole life. Something was happening to her that no one else could believe. Her own mind was turning, changing; her very thoughts were no longer her own, but dominated by some other creature, some force outside herself . . .

Her breathing quickened until she was nearly panting. The heat of her own body became stifling as the idea gained hold and the thing demanded a name, and the horror of it was so overwhelming that she ran up the stairs into the bathroom, locked the door, turned on the shower full force, pulled off her clothes and stepped inside, thinking only of water, water to cleanse her of that force which could only be evil. Nobody, nobody would ever believe her. Nobody would help. She screamed, inwardly, without sound, crying out with all the force she could muster, "No! I resist you! I will not believe, for my believing gives you space to grow. Devil! I resist you!"

Water poured over her head, her face, her body. Gradually Daria's breathing steadied, her hands hung limp at her sides. Exhausted, she stepped out of the shower and slowly dried herself. She felt numb, ashamed of her hysteria, but also empty inside. In all the world, there was nobody to help her.

Dressed in her cut-off jeans and plaid shirt, she set off toward the beach, moving doggedly, one foot after the other, without feeling. She wouldn't stay. She couldn't talk to Rob. She didn't even want to see him. She would just run up and tell him that there had been an emergency, and she couldn't stay.

7

*

She found Rob lying on a huge red beach towel just a few yards away from the pier.

"Smells fishy," Rob said, grinning, "but we get to watch the action. This morning a fellow reeled in a . . ." He stopped abruptly. "What's wrong?"

"Nothing." She felt awkward, standing there, and her fingers found the ends of her macrame belt, twisting the cords around and around.

"Sit down!" Rob propped himself up on one elbow. "Have I done something wrong? Are you mad at me?"

"No. Of course not. It's just—I don't think I can stay."

He nodded slowly, frowning. He turned his face away, toward the ocean. "Maybe," he said, "you want to stay a few minutes."

She sat down on the towel, putting her own things aside. In her mind echoes of the voice rushed at her like the crashing surf. *Love child!*

Still Rob remained silent, looking out at the sailboats in the distance.

"Rob," she began timidly, "it's nothing about you. I've had a problem. Could we just lie here for a while and not talk? I know it sounds crazy, but . . ."

"Sounds fine," he said calmly. "We'll just be still and listen to the surf."

They lay still for a long time, and Daria, almost unaware, turned her face away from Rob and felt the warm

57

sun on her cheeks, and once again the effortless tears came.

On and on she wept, lying motionless, scarcely thinking of anybody or anything. Presently she felt Rob's breath against her moist cheek. She saw his face very near hers. He whispered, "Want to talk about it?"

"Rob, you'll never want to see me again, and I don't blame you. I mean, what am I doing? I just lie here and c-cry! You know what the magazines say, and everybody, that when you go out you're supposed to laugh and be having—having f-f-*fun*, and I . . ."

Soberly Rob touched her cheek with his finger and said, "I am having fun."

He looked so earnest and so distressed that Daria laughed in spite of herself. "Oh, yeah, some fun, to watch me crying. I don't know what's wrong with me. I cry all the time. For no reason. But, well, also for reasons."

"You have been sick," he reminded her.

"It's not that." She sighed deeply. "It's something entirely different. There's nobody I can tell, either."

"Isn't Kelly your best friend?"

"Yes. She was." Again she felt that emptiness at her own use of the past tense, knowing it to be true. Oh, in time they might forget about what had happened last night, but it would never be the same again, because best friends must share things.

"What about your mom?" Rob asked.

Daria shook her head. For a long moment they looked at each other, Daria measuring the possible strength in him, in the firmness of his jaw, the strong, square fingers, and the lean but vigorous muscles of his arms. He had touched her cheek so gently, signifying—what? That he was a friend?

Softly she said, "Rob, I can't tell my mother things that

58

are personal—or unusual. If I try, she starts picking on me, or she doesn't understand."

He nodded, gazing at her without speaking.

As Daria looked at him, she imagined telling it. What possible words could she use, and how could she ever find the courage? What would he say? What might he do? No, no, you can't just tell people—people you hardly know—that a voice comes to you out of a dish, and it tells you things, awful things . . .

Suddenly she asked, "Are you my friend, Rob?"

"Yes. I'm your friend."

She half smiled. It was so stupid, so like little kids. What must he think of her? But he only nodded and took her hand and asked, "Do you want to tell me?"

"Yes." A few more tears came, quick and sparse, and she brushed them away. "Let's walk," Daria said, standing up. "I'd like to be walking while I tell you. I'd like to be by the water."

"All right," he said soberly. "Whatever you say."

They walked hand in hand, their steps in rhythm. Beneath their bare feet the sand was moist and pliant. Occasionally a fringe of white water touched their toes, but they walked on, oblivious, intent on listening and telling.

As Daria spoke, the events lost their nightmare quality, and for the first time appeared real and true. She told Rob everything, from winning the dish up to this morning, when Kelly had refused to admit what had happened.

"I guess," Daria said, breathing heavily, "it was just too impossible for her to accept. I guess if we saw that car just rise up and float away, we wouldn't believe our eyes, either."

"But you can accept it," Rob said.

"It was not the first time for me," Daria said. "It began slowly—I told you—just the suggestion of a voice at first, like a voice in my own mind, a conscience or some-

59

thing like that. It sort of came gradually, the smell, then the voice, then the shadows and the face.''

"I guess Kelly was scared out of her wits," Rob said.

"She gets very bad asthma," Daria said, nodding. "I'm sure her mother pounded it into her that there had to be a very natural explanation. And even if something weird did happen—I mean, if it could be *proved*—Mrs. Baxter would still try to talk Kelly out of it, if she thought it would hurt her. Kelly's terrific. I mean, she's the neatest person I know, but—but she can't take a lot of—of stress. She's not that strong."

He squeezed her hand slightly. "Most people aren't strong enough to take the kind of thing that's been happening to you," he said. There was admiration in his voice.

"You know," she said, looking down, "I haven't told anyone about this."

"Of course not! People would—"

"They'd say I was crazy! Or they'd laugh at me, or like Kelly, they'd panic. How come you're so different?"

He smiled. "Am I?"

"Well, I tell you this creepy story, and you *accept* it! I mean, Rob, do you think it's *possible*? How can such things happen? You don't seem to think it's weird."

"Maybe that's because I'm weird."

"What do you mean?" She eyed him sharply.

"This is your day, remember?" he said evasively. "We'll talk abut me some other time. Now, tell me about the face in the dish." He was intent and earnest, as if they were discussing something quite ordinary.

She murmured, "You really do believe me."

"Daria, I don't know what's possible. But I've heard that things like this do happen." In accord, they had stopped walking, and they sat down on the sand. "How could I help you if I didn't believe you? I want to help.

The face," he repeated. "Can you tell who it belongs to?"

"I'm not sure." Daria traced a stick figure in the sand—a head, body, legs and arms. In a way it was true. She wasn't positive. But her suspicions were growing stronger. Seemingly unrelated events were converging, memories blending with the new, strange phenomena. All were centered on Grandma. But it was too preposterous to see the face of someone who'd been dead for years, and she couldn't bring herself to tell Rob. It made her feel like a ghoul.

Rob asked, "Could it have been your own face?"

"My reflection!" she exclaimed. "It if were as simple as that . . ."

"I don't mean your reflection. I mean . . ." He groped for words, "maybe part of yourself, the way you were earlier. Or as you might be in the future."

"No." Daria smoothed out the sand. "What you're saying sounds like science fiction. A time warp or something. I don't think it's anything like that. It's like—like something is wrong, suddenly with—with my *brain*."

He smiled slightly. "Just because a thing is different," he said, "doesn't necessarily mean it's *wrong*. Has anything like this ever happened to you before?" From his pocket Rob took a roll of Life Savers. He popped the red one into her mouth, leaned forward and very tenderly, very lightly, touched her lips with his.

She smiled slightly. "Thanks."

"For what?" He was grinning.

"For the candy, of course. It helps." She added, "I haven't eaten since breakfast."

"Want to go get something?"

She shook her head. "We've got work to do." The word "work" seemed strangely appropriate. Her eyes and her neck felt strained and tense, as if all her energy were concentrated in her brain. Rob, suddenly, seemed more like a teacher than a friend as he questioned her. He repeated, "Has anything like this happened to you before?"

"No." Daria said the word, but without conviction, for even as she spoke her thoughts began drifting back to other times, and slowly she admitted, "Little things, not important, like knowing when my mother was going to bring home a surprise. Or I'd know if someone was going to drop in unexpectedly. I never thought about it. Maybe I figured everybody knows things like that." She shrugged, then faced Rob. "But not everyone does know these things, do they?"

"No." He stared at her almost sadly. "But some people have an ability. ESP. You know, ways to pick up things."

Wrapped in her memories, Daria scarcely heard him. "At school I always know when the teacher's going to call on me. When I was little, I'd pretend there was a wall around me, so she couldn't call on me, and then she never did. You could call it intuition."

"Everybody has some kind of intuition," Rob agreed.

"But that's not like seeing a face in a dish. That's . . ."

She broke off, her voice seeming to merge into a haze of memories that pulled her back through many years. As if a curtain had been lifted, suddenly she felt the terrible ache of a grief that had been hidden away; it was as if she were there again.

"I was only five," she whispered, her voice nearly a singsong. "My grandma died, and I knew she was dead. I knew, but there was no way for me to know. No possible, logical way. We were in California. But I could see her, plain as anything, in her old house in Missouri. Two big trees on either side of the porch. She sat there in the hammock. It creaked while she rocked back and forth. The wind—the wind blew the leaves from the trees down onto the porch, and they swirled around her feet. She put her hand up to her throat. She wiped her forehead with her apron. She was breathing hard, hurting, her arms hurting as if somebody had tied them down with a rubber hose. Then a weight came down, hard, on her chest. I screamed! My mother ran in, and I was screaming and sobbing. 'Grandma's dead!' I yelled. 'Grandma's dead!' "

Daria could hardly swallow. She whispered, "Do you have another Life Saver?"

"Sure."

She put it into her mouth and concentrated on the sweet taste, making it bring her back. "I'd forgotten. It was awful."

Rob asked, "Was she dead?"

Daria nodded. "That night we got a phone call from Grandma's neighbor. He'd gone over to bring her a sackful of apples. He found her dead in the hammock. The doctor said it was her heart." She shivered, as if a chill wind had blown across the beach.

"I remember too," Daria continued in a low voice, "how my mother looked at me when we found out Grandma was really dead. She was horrified."

"Well, her mother had just died . . ."

"It wasn't that. It was because of me, because of my knowing. It was as if she couldn't stand to come near me." She closed her eyes against the tears that threatened. "Sometimes she's like that. Like, she won't even use the things I give her. I wanted to give her the dish. I wonder what would have happened if she'd taken it?"

"I was thinking," Rob said, "you could just get rid of it." He stared at her challengingly, intently. "Just throw it away."

"I know. I've thought of smashing it." She gave him a slight, crooked smile. "Somehow I can't. I've got to find out what all this is about."

Rob grinned at her and took her hand, drawing her up.

"Let's walk back. I'll bet you're starved. I didn't pack a lunch after all. But I'll get you a hamburger at Polo Joe's."

Daria nodded. "My mother was really shook when I gave her that perfume, that Dew Delight, because it was Grandma's favorite." They began to walk. "That whole thing was weird, too, the way I found that perfume in the drugstore just a few weeks before my Mom's birthday. The minute I walked into the store, I could smell it, and I picked out the right tester from eight of them, without even thinking. I was drawn to that perfume. I loved it right away. Could it be that I actually remembered the smell from the time I was a baby?"

"I guess it could be a coincidence," Rob said. "Lots of people happen to like the same perfume."

"I never saw my grandmother after we left Missouri when I was one and a half. It's so strange, Rob. I keep remembering things I couldn't normally remember—even things I never actually knew. Like that song."

"Maybe it isn't a matter of remembering. Maybe it's all new information."

"From where?" She grimaced. "I'm not a radio receiver!"

Rob laughed. "I don't know. I once read about a man who did get radio signals through a tooth that had just been filled."

Daria chuckled, opened her mouth. "Look, Rob, no cavities."

"About remembering," he added, "I could ask my dad how far back babies can usually remember."

"Why would he know?"

"He's a psychologist. He studies things like that." Rob hesitated, slowing his steps, too, until he stopped and turned his face half away from her. "He's been doing some research into—psychic phenomena."

Daria, standing stock-still, only stared at him.

"Precognition," Rob explained, facing her. "ESP. Stuff like that."

They looked at each other for a long moment, silently, and then Daria said in a voice that was low and almost fierce with urgency, "I don't want you to tell your dad anything about me, do you hear?"

He retreated, mistaking her alarm for anger, and snapped back, "Well, then, I won't!"

"Rob," she demanded, "do you honestly believe that this is all just a coincidence? All these things that have been happening to me, and now here I am telling you, and your dad just *happens* to be into ESP and psychic phenomena—and you just happened to be the one who gave me the dish that started it all. Do you really think it's all just coincidence?"

He seemed hardly to be listening, and she grasped his arm, aware that she was talking too loudly, nearly shouting at him. He turned slowly to look at her, shaking his head.

"I'm sorry," she whispered. "I didn't mean to attack you. It just seems like there's a whole conspiracy . . ."

"And I'm part of it?" He began to walk rapidly, his jaw set tightly, and she had to hurry to keep up.

"I didn't mean—I'm not saying you're tricking me or anything. It's just so strange."

He took her hand again, and they walked together. "Maybe," he said, speaking slowly, as if to clarify his own thoughts, "maybe everything is coincidence. A million to one chance, like winning a lottery or getting hit by a meteor, and you've just stumbled into one of those rare, freak occurrences."

He took a deep breath, then determinedly continued. "Or maybe nothing is ever a coincidence. Maybe everything that happens to us fits into a plan. Maybe it was no accident that I was in your English class, and then we met at the carnival, and you chose to confide in me. Because

65

I can really understand what you're going through, Daria, since I—"

He broke off abruptly and went to the water tap to rinse the sand from his feet. Hurriedly, Daria followed.

"Rob, what do you mean? Why can you understand?"

He dried his feet with the edge of his towel, then looked up at her. "Daria, I think you should do some reading. You'll see that other people have gone through things like this, and things that are even—even stranger."

"Have you, Rob?" She looked up at him pleadingly. "Have you ever experienced anything like this?"

"No. Not like this," he said vaguely. "Hey, I'm starved! Let's go eat."

Daria lay on her stomach on her rose beige bedroom rug. It was where she did her best thinking, gazing down at the worn, faded fabric.

It seemed incredible that a night would pass when she didn't talk to Kelly on the telephone. Ordinarily they would have discussed every detail of her date with Rob. But not now. Unless they could talk about last night, they would never be able to confide in each other again. The kids at school, so used to seeing them together, would begin to wonder what had happened. Daria was sure of one thing; Kelly would never tell them about last night. It wasn't in her to do that.

Daria rolled over onto her back, staring up at the ceiling, an acoustic substance composed of bumpy specks of plaster. Strange, how calm she felt, how peaceful. Had anyone suggested that Kelly would do this to her, she would have expected to be furious for days. But she lay contentedly on the rug, thinking of the ocean and the sand and Rob. Rob believed her. He didn't think she was crazy. Rob liked her. She knew he did. And he had kissed her.

Dreamily Daria reached for her sketch pad. With light

pencil strokes she began to draw the old-fashioned porch with its sagging floorboards and fancy railing, the two large trees, the hammock with its awning.

Above the drawing of the porch, enclosed in a circle as in a locket, Daria attempted to sketch a face. In her mind's eye she saw the features only vaguely. She erased the lines, about to begin again, when the telephone rang, and a moment later her mother called, "Daria! It's for you."

As she ran down the stairs, her mother added, "Daria, you must make it clear to your friends that I won't allow phone calls after ten o'clock."

Daria brushed past her. "Who is it?"

"A boy."

Daria sat down on the kitchen floor, her back against the wall. "Hi," she said softly, conscious that her mother could be listening from the living room.

Rob's voice, too, was low.

"Is this Madame Minerva?" Daria teased. "If so, speak up."

"The same," he said. "I just wondered—I had a good time today. It was nice at the beach."

Priscilla came to rub against her leg, purring, and Daria gently stroked the cat's head. "I had a good time, too. I've been thinking about it. You asked me a question—"

"You don't owe me any answers," he said quickly.

"I want to tell you! It was my grandmother's face," she whispered. "Does that give you the creeps?"

He countered, "Does it give *you* the creeps?"

"I mean the dead one," she said. "From Missouri."

"I know." He seemed to move closer to the telephone, as if his lips would touch her cheek. "Daria, are you scared?"

Her mother called out sharply, "Daria! Time to get off the phone!"

"In a minute!" Daria called back. "Rob, I feel so odd about all this. What'll I do?"

Cautiously he asked, "Do you want me to ask my dad?"

"No. I've got to think. If it is my—if it could be . . ." She paused, and a great shiver began at the back of her neck, running down her spine. "Rob, do you realize what we're talking about? It's ghosts we're talking about."

"Yes," Rob said.

"Rob, do you really believe in—?"

"Daria!" her mother cried. "Get off that phone!"

"Maybe," Rob said, "there's a reasonable explanation."

"That's what I've got to find out." Her heart was pounding. "Maybe there's some way to do this. Maybe someone alive is doing it to me."

"That's possible," Rob admitted. "But who?"

"Daria, I'm not asking you again!" Her mother appeared in the kitchen, angrily shaking her finger.

Daria forced her tone to be brisk. " 'Bye, Rob. Sorry, Mom." She hurried away, upstairs, the question repeating itself in her mind.

In the night, even as she slept, the question loomed before her. Who? Who? Shapes and faces floated eerily in and out of her dreams, along with the certainty that there were ways to accomplish such illusions. The ways of the magician, the circus performer, the con artist. There were ways to create illusions—like Disneyland, like the Fun House, like special effects in movies. . . .

But who? Who would do such a thing, and why? Hateful neighbors. Former friends turned enemies. The delivery boy with a grudge against her. A psychopath on the loose. A complete stranger, or someone she knew intimately. . . .

Yes, it could be. It could be someone very close. The person doing it had to be close enough to slip easily into her room, someone who knew her habits and her fears. . . .

No. She must not think of it. Turning in her sleep, straining against the thought, Daria struggled and twisted, but the thought gained upon her as she slept. Like some stealthy creature, it gained upon her until it rose to overwhelm her. She awakened suddenly, wide-eyed and staring, flooded with an awful certainty and one word on her lips, "Mother."

It could even be her own mother.

8

*

The last two weeks of April it rained almost continually. It was a slow, steady rain, falling like a heavy mist, gray and forlorn, making the mind sluggish. The rain seemed endless and pointless, like Daria's searching.

Round and round the same questions hammered through her brain, leaving her without energy for anything else. What was happening to her? Was it real or did she imagine it? If real, was it an illusion created by someone who hated her? If so, who?

If it was no illusion, she had to find the source. Did the vision come from some secret place within her own mind? Or did it come from outside herself? Was it evil? Then she must find some way to protect herself. If good, what was its purpose? And regardless of all these other considerations, how, ever again, would she be able to feel any freedom and control over her own life?

The questions claimed Daria's attention completely. In math class the teacher's dry voice crackled on, rising to call out in sarcasm, "If our friend, Daria The Dreamer, doesn't mind, we shall continue . . ." Daria only sighed. She didn't care, didn't want to know, couldn't possibly focus her thoughts on numbers.

In English it was the same. She sat before her open book staring at the pages until the print ran together, forming shadows that billowed and crooned, "Love child!"

Rob would wait for her before class, and they'd stand

out in the hall talking together before the bell rang. Like two people playing a part from a script, they talked about silly, inconsequential things. Rob always brought Life Savers in his pocket, and, like a ritual, just before they went in he'd pop one into her mouth.

On cue, Daria would smile at him and say, "Thanks."

"For what?" he'd counter.

Then she'd say, "For the kiss, of course."

But it was only a moment of banter, filling time that could not be given to the important things—not yet.

"I have a lot of thinking to do, Rob," she told him, her voice soft and serious. "I'm not really—not myself. I feel almost as if I've been very sick for a long time, that I've got to recuperate. Can you understand that? I can't seem to get used to the idea that . . ."

Slowly he nodded and put his hand up on the wall above her, as if to enfold her, but without touching. "I won't try to rush you," he said.

"I know that, Rob, and I thank you for it. I wish . . ."

"It's OK. You just do what you have to do. I'll wait until you're through doing it, OK?"

She was grateful for Rob. Everyone else she knew seemed to be drawing away from her. When Daria came upon her friends, even if they said nothing, she detected a stiffness in their bearing. Sometimes they acted suddenly shy, or they'd glance up guiltily, as if they'd been talking about her.

Sometimes Daria overheard snatches of conversation, and it hurt.

". . . obviously they had a fight . . ."

"I'm on Kelly's side, aren't you?"

". . . gotten kinda stuck-up lately . . ."

". . . 'cause she's going with that boy."

They were changing. Or was she the one? She was constantly forgetting things—to start the roast, to wash her

71

hair, even to feed Priscilla, until late in the evening the cat would rub up against her leg, then sit before her with a wide-eyed, reproachful, "Mee-ow!"

Filled with remorse, Daria would bring the cat into her bed at night, stroking her and murmuring softly, "Oh, Miss Priss, I wish you could help me. Everything is so strange."

Then her mother would fuss about the cat being in the bed, until her scolding took in all Daria's other faults, too, her untidiness, forgetfulness, and finally, "You're staying up much too late, Daria! You ought to budget your time better. You'll make yourself sick."

"I am already sick!" she muttered under her breath, and for an instant she even wavered over the thought of telling her mother, getting it out in the open once and for all. But the idea was shattered as a succession of memories leaped before her. How very often in the past she had confessed to some trouble, only to be blamed for it.

She didn't know whether or not her mother had heard. But much later in the night Peg tiptoed into Daria's room. Daria lay on her side, still awake, eyes open just enough to see her mother cross the room and walk over to the bureau. For several minutes Peg stood there, looking first out the window, then down into the dish.

She knows, Daria thought, her heart pounding with dread. She knows, either because she is like me, somehow, or because she is doing it to me. And if she is doing it, it could only be because there is something terribly wrong with her. Or—a small voice within her countered maliciously—there is something wrong with you, something horribly wrong, that you would accuse your mother of such things.

Which was it? After school, Daria would walk around town in the rain until her shoes were soaked through, thinking, thinking. There seemed to be no refuge from her questions or from the wet streets and wind-tossed trees and the cold gloom. Then one day, impulsively, she boarded the Beach Drive bus and fifteen minutes later stood before the large stucco library. From then on Daria went to the library nearly every day.

She walked among the shelves, staring at the titles, almost afraid to look. What if the books had no answers for her, either? But she began, standing first in the dim aisle, moving eventually to a small table in a secluded alcove. There she piled the books beside her and started, in earnest, to study. To her amazement, it was all recorded. Other people had asked the same questions. There were words for such experiences as hers. What began with sorcery, magic and witchcraft, blended into such topics as drug use, altered states of consciousness, psychology, ESP, psychic phenomena, meditation, reincarnation. It was all in print, the incredible made possible.

Through the ages, ordinary people like herself had experienced things they could not explain. Now, several great universities were probing into such things as ESP. What was once called sheer superstitious nonsense was being verified in scientific studies.

But there was another side, too. Nearly every book gave warning. Beware of charlatans. Be skeptical of strange unnatural occurrences or of people who claim to have all the answers. People are prey to illusion.

Prey to illusion—was that it? Was she being deceived, somehow?

Her mother was pleased that Daria was studying. "High time," she said with a sniff, "that you quit fooling around and got down to business!" Daria smiled to herself at the irony of it. If her mother only knew! Once Daria had bought a paperback book on palmistry, and her mother had nearly had a fit.

"If you're going to spend good money on this kind of

trash," she had yelled, "I'm going to cut your allowance! Filling your head with nonsense . . . I thought you had more brains." She had fumed and sputtered; so angry that Daria was aghast. "Some people actually fall for this stuff," Peg said bitterly, "and it can ruin their whole—" She had stopped abruptly, her teeth clenched, and Daria had said nothing. She had stopped trying to figure out her mother's sudden moods.

Now Daria simply covered the library books with brown paper, and when she was finished reading, shoved them under her bed. As she read, sometimes she would look up, suddenly alert to some presence. But she shrugged it off. It was only her mother getting ready for bed, or Priscilla scratching at the banister, or the rain on the roof. Beneath this logic, however, lay her persistent awareness of a strange, pervasive fragrance. By turns, it faded and grew stronger. Sometimes she awakened in the middle of the night feeling as if she had been drenched in Dew Delight. And one night she knew she could wait no longer.

With quick, light steps she rushed to her wall, pressed her ear against it. Yes, it had to be her mother. She was surely clever enough, and for some twisted motive, relentless enough to drive her own daughter mad.

Standing close to the wall, Daria held her breath. She heard nothing. Slowly, softly, she opened her door and moved out into the hall, certain now that it was Peg. For what motive? her logical mind demanded. For hatred, Daria answered herself. She hates me, because we're so different, because I've tied her down all these years, because she's had to be responsible for me. If I were put away in a hospital, she'd be rid of me for good.

Daria moved down the hall toward her mother's door. Priscilla, snug in her basket, stretched out her paws but did not get up.

For several moments Daria waited there. In the silence she could visualize Peg perfectly, standing in the middle of the room wearing her white nightgown, squeezing the atomizer, sending the perfume spray to float from her window into Daria's. Her figure would be slightly bent, her head thrown back in mad, ecstatic celebration over this, her final revenge.

With one swift motion Daria flung open her mother's door. In that moment she cried out her accusation, "You!"

But she saw her mother's body huddled in sleep. Peg sat up, blinking, and she stammered, "Daria? What's wrong? Are you sick, honey?"

Daria's breath felt locked in her throat. "I'm OK," she stammered. "I wasn't feeling very well. But I'm OK now."

She stood a moment longer, breathing deeply to try to inhale the fragrance, but it was not there. Sharply she asked, "Have you opened that bottle of Dew Delight perfume I gave you?"

"Daria, for heaven's sake, it's four in the morning and you ask me about perfume! Why do you do this to me?" Peg's voice rose. Then she flung herself down and buried her face in her pillow. Noiselessly Daria retreated, closing the door behind her.

In her room again, she turned on the light, shivering and trembling with relief. A strange joy flooded over her as she realized that whatever was happening to her, at least her mother was not responsible. She had not realized she was smiling and weeping at the same time, until she caught her full reflection in the mirror.

Now she moved closer, gazing at her face calmly, deliberately, saying her name to herself. Daria. I am Daria Peterson. My face is not strange. My eyes are clear. This is not the face of a wild and crazy person. I am Daria Peterson, and I did see a vision in a dish. It was not an illusion. It was not simply my imagination, because Kelly saw it too. I don't know how it happened, and I don't know why. But I will find out.

For an instant her resolve wavered. *You?* a small voice mocked from within her. *You had a vision? Like St. Joan? Like Mohammed and the Virgin Mary? Like saints? Oh, come on, Daria.*

Maybe it was not a religious vision, she told herself emphatically, but it was a vision. And it was Grandma.

Daria opened her door and whispered, "Psst!" Instantly Priscilla came rushing into her arms. She brought the cat to her bed. Priscilla settled herself close, and the soft warmth and Priscilla's gentle purring sent Daria drifting into sleep.

The dream came at once. Down floated one angel, taking its place at Daria's head. The others settled themselves in their places. They were clothed in silvery stuff. She could sense the softness of their bodies and the strength of their purpose. Their purpose was to bring her love.

With that awareness the Grandma appeared, life-size, standing not on the floor but in the space between floor and ceiling, her body sharply etched against moonlight from the window.

"Here I am, Daria," She said.

"I wanted you before. Why didn't you come sooner?" In her dream Daria's voice sounded reproachful, and she regretted it.

"You wouldn't have been able to deal with it, that's why." She pursed her lips as if to hide a smile. "You're stubborn," She continued, "but you're getting there. Now, pay attention. Understand, Daria, that you have much to learn."

"Everyone tells me that."

"Maybe because it's true," She said briskly. "To begin with, you already know about color and shape, but you

76

don't yet recognize the importance of it. You see things in color. For you, color is a whole separate dimension.''

''How did you know that?''

''It's a good thing,'' She continued, ''but you ought to devote yourself to this gift. There are many ways to use your talent, if you're willing to risk trying something new.''

''You mean I ought to paint more?''

''Good heavens!'' She chuckled. ''That's the trouble with people. Always trying to boil everything down to specifics—ask a question, get an answer. Haven't you ever had *ideas* that seemed to demand more of you? Pause, sometimes, to catch those ideas, those little inspirations. Once, I believe, you had the courage to paint a purple owl with four eyes, sitting on a cookie jar. You were very young.'' She sighed. ''Perhaps we lose some of our spontaneity as we mature. Pity.''

In the dream, Daria frowned. What on earth was She driving at? Daria asked, ''Do you think I should take art in summer school?''

''There you go again, Daria. I won't solve problems for you.'' She drew herself up proudly. ''I'm not one of those plaster ladies grinning from inside a glass booth at the fair. You know, put in a dime, get a printed card with your fortune. You've got the wrong idea.''

''Well, how am I supposed to know how to talk to a ghost?'' Daria snapped. ''They don't teach us that at school.''

''Sassy,'' She observed. ''Most girls your age are.''

''Why aren't you in the dish?'' Daria asked. ''I thought you had to be in the dish.''

She laughed gaily. ''I don't *live* in that dish. Nobody lives in a dish. Would you?''

''That's silly. Of course I wouldn't. But I'm a person.''

''How tiresome you are!'' She said, but merrily. ''That's

the trouble, you see. You keep thinking of yourself only as a person. As if you were no more than a bundle of skin and bones, muscles and nerves. You," She said, "are much more than your body."

"You mean soul?"

"Call it that, if you like. I'm not sure what it really is. Just because I was in the dish doesn't mean I know everything. I'm still learning, too. By the way, since you're so concerned about that body of yours, you should cut down on French fries. Horrible for your skin."

"Is that what you came to tell me?" Daria scoffed. "You needn't have bothered. My mom tells me that all the time."

"Oh, yes, your mother. Let's talk about her."

Two of the angels floated slightly upwards, then nestled down among the covers again.

"Your mother is a good woman," She said, "but too practical."

Daria murmured, "They say it's smart to be practical."

"*They?*" She laughed. "Oh, yes, I have heard a great deal about a group called 'They.' A lot of meddlers, 'They' are! Well, one should be practical, but only to a point. One must also be open to new ideas. Like your friend, Maude. Tell her. She and her mother . . ."

"I don't know any Maude," said Daria.

"Tell Maude. The Irish one. The one who wears green. *You* know."

"I don't know any Maude," Daria insisted.

"I never argue," She said with great dignity. "My point is, if you were utterly practical, you would also be rigid, and we would not be having this little chat. If you were not ready to listen, believe me, we couldn't have gotten even this far."

"But—but this is . . ." Daria stammered.

78

"You must realize that we've progressed, from the dish to—this."

"But this is only a dream!" Daria exclaimed.

"Only a dream?" She fluttered her hands in agitation. "Only a dream, you say!" She seemed to move closer, Her body bending toward Daria as She challenged, "Why don't you ask *her*, then. Make her tell you the truth. If you ask her outright, she will have to tell you. I know her. She cannot lie."

Baffled, Daria murmured, "You mean my mother? Ask her what?"

"You'll know how to manage it," She said briskly. The silver stuff of her began to snap and sparkle. "You ask her," She said, "and enjoy yourself with Maude!"

There came a strange little popping sound, like a light bulb burning out. Then She was gone.

9

*

Sometimes when the telephone rang, and Daria ran to answer it, nobody was there. Was it only her imagination? Or a prankster? Or was this symbolic of that other unearthly "caller," taunting her, making her doubt her reason.

The phone used to ring constantly. She and Kelly used to call back and forth, talking about what they'd wear to school the next day, whether they'd bring lunch or buy it, and just talking and laughing. Now Kelly hardly even said hello anymore. Sometimes Daria saw her walking with Charlie Lacey, and then Kelly lifted her head and looked right past Daria.

Rob was the only person who called her. Once or twice a week he'd phone. But their conversations were guarded, almost empty. He seemed timid, waiting for Daria to begin.

For several days afterward she pondered that strange nighttime conversation with the silvery, ethereal Grandma. *Was* it a dream? It had been very much *like* a dream, but not altogether, not quite. Dream people don't talk back that way, or issue instructions, or insist that they are real.

When Rob phoned late one night, after Peg had gone to sleep, Daria decided to tell him. She sat down on the kitchen floor, back pressed against the wall, and she whispered, "Can I see you tomorrow?"

"Sure. Want to have lunch together?"

"Yes," she whispered. "I had a dream that seemed so real—so different. I've been reading about dreams and what they might mean. I've been reading a lot."

"I know," he said. "I see you with all those books under your arm. Do you ever sleep?" He sounded concerned.

She laughed. "I just told you—I've been dreaming. Would you ask your dad for me—that is, would you tell him about my—my whole experience? And the dream later, after I've told you. I still smell the perfume. Could a person remember a smell from so long ago and have it seem real? Could you remember a person that you only knew when you were a baby?"

"I'll ask my dad at breakfast," Rob said. "See you tomorrow."

All through the morning she watched the clock impatiently, until at last the lunch bell rang, and she and Rob walked together to the grassy field behind the school.

They sat down. Daria began plucking out bits of wild grass to hide her nervousness. "Did you tell your dad about me?"

"Yes. He was very interested."

"He doesn't think I'm crazy?"

"No. Do you?"

Daria laughed. "You sound like a shrink yourself."

"My dad always gives answers by telling about various theories," Rob began. "He said some psychiatrists say that dreams are just your wishes and desires, acted out in your mind. They're a safety valve. You get to do things in dreams that you can't do while you're awake, so the dream gives you relief."

"It was Grandma," Daria said.

"In your dream?"

She nodded. Then she told it, as much for her own sake as for Rob's. "It was not part of me, my thoughts or my subconscious. It was," she hesitated, "it was *like* a dream, but more than a dream. I think She was a separate entity."

"I see." Rob sounded neither surprised nor perplexed.

"You do," she stated, half smiling. "OK, now the way I figure it, a baby does experience feelings. Maybe it could remember them, too, especially if they—"

"If they were very strong feelings," Rob broke in.

"Yes, that's what my dad said. One theory is that feelings and experiences are imprinted on a baby's mind, even before he knows the words for them. Later, that memory could be brought back, triggered by something—a fragrance or a place . . ."

"Maybe that's why sometimes a new place seems so familiar," Daria said.

Rob continued. "My dad also told me some people even claim to remember what it felt like to be *born* and before that."

"Oh, come on," she said.

"My dad didn't say it was true," Rob said with a shrug. "He just said it was *possible*."

She watched Rob take several waxed bags from his lunch sack and remembered. "I didn't bring a lunch."

"No problem," Rob said, munching on a carrot. "Wait till you see this. My mom always thinks I'll starve between lunch and dinner." As Rob spoke he laid out two sandwiches, pretzels, an apple, a banana and cookies.

Daria smiled as she took the proffered sandwich. "With all this, how come you're still thin?"

"From worrying," he said soberly, meeting her gaze, "about you." Then he grinned. "I'm glad you're back."

"Am I?"

"Definitely. You've been gone, you know. Missing in action."

"I know," she said softly. "I had to get away and think

and find out. . . . There's just one more thing I have to do. I have to find out whether it's true.''

"What's true?"

"What the face in the dish said. About me. That I'm a . . .''

"Oh.'' Rob sighed. "And you think it will help to know?''

"Rob, I know that the visions are real. Nobody is tricking me. Now, they could either be just some silly phenomena—like you said, a coincidence that really has nothing to do with my life, like a poltergeist . . .''

"A capricious ghost,'' Rob murmured, nodding.

"Or, there is a reason for all this. That means I'd be getting information, messages . . .''

"From whom?'' Rob leaned forward intently. "From the other—''

"It doesn't matter,'' Daria said quickly. "The point is, I have to find out whether what *She* says is true. Then, maybe, I can try to figure out why this is happening. Maybe there is something I'm supposed to do, don't you see?''

"Yes, I see,'' he said, taking her hand and holding it tightly. "Are you scared?''

She nodded. "In the dream, She told me to ask my mother. She wasn't specific, but I know what She meant. That dream was so real, Rob!''

"My dad says that dreams come from the subconscious.'' He paused, looking to a distance.

She confronted him. "What do *you* believe, Rob?''

"I'm not sure. I've thought about it a lot.''

"Why, Rob?'' She met his eyes, pleading. "How are you involved in this? You're the only one who has any idea of what I'm going through. How come?''

"I've had some experiences,'' he said slowly. "Not quite like yours, but—frightening, too. It's what made my

83

dad get interested in parapsychology. So I know how you feel, I guess. I know you need time to be alone and think and get used to the idea, because I—'' He stopped abruptly, stood up and said, "The bell just rang."

"I want to know, Rob," she said.

He nodded. "I want to tell you, too, when we have time. How about meeting me at the beach next Sunday?"

"Yes. About noon? At Twinkie's?"

They walked back together, their hands touching lightly, until they neared the building. "Sunday," she repeated, her heart racing. Sunday—Sunday—by then perhaps she'd have another answer, too.

All the rest of the day she thought only of Rob and of Sunday. Preoccupied, she bumped into people in the hallways, and at the library later that afternoon, when Nan McGraw sat right down beside her, Daria didn't even notice until she spoke. The voice made Daria jump as if she'd touched a high voltage wire.

"Good grief! What's wrong, Daria? You're so jumpy."

"Oh—I was just concentrating." Daria's face felt flushed, and Nan chuckled softly.

"I guess you were thinking about Rob," she said. "I saw the two of you having lunch together. He looked at you as if nobody else existed in the whole world."

Daria only smiled. It seemed silly to talk about Rob the way Kelly used to talk about Charlie Lacey—mooning and dreaming, inventing things. Rob was different. He was real, and a friend, and . . .

"You really like him a lot, don't you," Nan stated.

"Yes. I . . ."

"*Magic and the Human Mind!*" Nan had picked up one of the books, and now excitedly read the titles aloud. "*The Sixth Sense. Your Many Lives And Infinite Realities.*" She turned to Daria, her eyes wide in amazement. "I didn't

84

know you were into this kind of stuff, Daria. This is heavy. Is it for a report?''

"Yes. No—actually, it's just for my—my own interest.''

"Wow!'' Nan seemed overwhelmed with the discovery. "I didn't know you—that is, I never even saw you at the library before. My mom and I are both nuts about this kind of thing, and sometimes she brings home books. My dad says we're both out of our tree, but then, he's a scientist, and you know how *they* are.''

Daria had never heard Nan speaking so quickly or so excitedly. She sat back, surprised and pleased at Nan's sudden exuberance.

"This stuff is really interesting, and my mother. . . . Good grief, there's her horn. Want a ride home?''

"Sure!''

On the way home they talked and laughed, and Mrs. McGraw turned to Daria and said, smiling, "Why don't you come over sometime, Daria?''

And Nan added, "Maybe you could spend the night.''

It was all so casual, and no definite date was made, but Daria somehow felt that the day had been eventful, and that something important had occurred.

Her mother had gone out to the all-night market, to pick up some milk for breakfast. "It's that damn cat!'' she had shouted behind her. "You give our milk to that damn cat!''

Daria sat on the living room floor. Priscilla lay beside her, rolled into a ball. The TV was on, a steady droning sound and moving pictures that seemed vague and illusive compared to that sharp, lifelike picture in Daria's mind. The sketch pad lay in her lap. She had been doodling with the charcoal pencil. A drawing had taken shape, first the fancy grillwork on an old-fashioned porch, then the two tall trees with their large leaves, some falling and swirl-

85

ing in the wind, some settling around the old woman's shoes . . .

"Don't you have any homework, Daria?"

She had not heard her mother come in, but Priscilla had, and now the cat lay crouched on the back of the easy chair, unblinking and almost fierce.

Peg's shadow fell across the page of Daria's sketch pad. Peg's voice, harsh with reproof, said, "You fool around too much."

How tall she seemed, how hard, standing up in front of Daria. From her place on the floor, Daria could see the hem of her mother's dress, the angular, shadowed cut of her jaw, the slender throat, hollows beneath the eyes.

"I need some new pastels, Mother."

"We'll see. I should think you'd need to spend more time on your studies. And I've been meaning to talk to you about summer school. I'm not going to have you just hanging around all summer with nothing to do. So, you sign up for some real course, none of this craftsy stuff. Take something like business math—"

"Mom, why didn't we ever see Grandma?"

"Business math and typing. If you learn to type, you can—"

"Why didn't we even write to her?"

"Daria, for heaven's sake, what's coming over you? You know your grandmother is dead. What's all this sudden fascination with people who've been dead for years?"

"I mean, before she died. We never saw her."

"Obviously, I couldn't afford to go traipsing off to Missouri at the drop of a hat. I had obligations, don't you know?" Harshly she added, "We went to the funeral."

"I didn't."

"You were too little. Daria, what's wrong with you? You went back to Missouri with me. I didn't just abandon you. During the funeral you stayed with friends."

86

"I didn't get to see her."

"For God's sake, you wanted to see a *dead person? A corpse?*"

"My grandmother!" Daria shouted. "I wanted to see her!"

In a single, furious motion, Peg whirled around, and her shoes made stamping, angry sounds as she walked through the apartment, through the kitchen, slammed the door, then up into her bedroom, slamming that door, too, so that the walls shook.

For a few seconds Daria waited, motionless. Then, relentlessly, she followed. At Peg's door she did not wait until her knock was answered. She opened the door and in a low voice she said, "Tell me about my father."

Peg's face, pale in the faint light from her dressing table lamp, drew taut. For an instant she gazed straight at Daria. Then she sighed. "Honey, I'm dead-tired tonight. I want to take a bath. Let's talk about it some other time, OK? I've got to do my nails before tomorrow. And my hair's a mess."

She picked up her brush, ran it through her hair a couple of times, then began to search for her nail file and buffer, frantically opening and closing the dresser drawers, shaking her head, as if the loss of these small implements foreshadowed disaster.

"Mother," Daria persisted, "tell me about my father. How old was he when I was born?"

Wearily Peg went to the window, lifted the curtain slightly and looked out to the stars. "Very well," she said, her tone dull and resigned. "He was twenty-three, and he was killed five months before you were born."

"How old was he when you and he were married?"

"It was a year before he was killed. He was twenty-two."

"And you were twenty?"

"I was twenty."

"When you were married?"

"Yes. I've told you a hundred times."

Slowly Daria approached her mother, intently watching her face. "You know," she said, "I remember that picture of my father. You showed it to me a long time ago. There were two pictures, that's all. Just two pictures of him. One was taken at some amusement park. He was standing behind a cartoon of Popeye. You know the kind—with the face cut out. For years I thought my daddy was Popeye. Isn't that a laugh?"

"Honey, why do you do this to yourself? Why don't you just let it alone. Listen, let's go out for a walk. It's nice outside. We'll walk by the pier, get an ice cream—"

"No, Mother. I want to see his picture."

"Oh, honey, I don't even know where it is. Daria, you're making me feel really rotten. You must understand, it hasn't been easy for me. I've tried to adjust. I don't see what good all this . . ."

Thoughts whirled and exploded in Daria's mind, like Fourth of July pinwheels. Now. She must learn the truth now. She could hear the harshness of her own breathing, and beneath it the spiteful taunt, "Love child!"

"I want to see his picture," she said.

Peg turned from the window and walked back to her bureau. "I told you," she said briskly. "I don't even know where it is."

"If he'd been my husband," Daria said, "I'd wear his picture in a locket around my neck. I wouldn't lose it."

Peg's cheeks got that mottled look. Her nostrils flared. "Daria, must you be deliberately cruel? Wearing a picture around one's neck doesn't prove anything. I loved my husband—"

"It's a lie."

For a moment all movement ceased. The statement

88

might have been screamed down into a canyon, as somehow the accusing words echoed and re-echoed. "It's a lie."

Again came Daria's voice, calm and steady, colder than she herself had ever heard it. "You were never married to him. I'm just a bastard. And that makes you a—"

In one instant Peg leaped forth, and in that instant struck. Daria recoiled, her body surging out into the small landing, and as she fell she struck her head against the railing with a blinding force.

"Daria?" Peg came slowly toward her, staring down. "Are you all right? Daria, listen, I didn't mean to—that was a terrible thing to say. How could you have?"

Dazed, Daria stared up at her mother. "It's true," she said tonelessly. "It's true, I know. Otherwise you wouldn't have hit me. You and my father were never married. If you were, you could show me the marriage certificate."

Again in that silence between them, time seemed to stretch beyond measurement of clocks or any physical forces. As if they had confronted one another forever, they were locked in combat, Daria still down where she had fallen, Peg standing over her.

At last Peg turned away. "I loved him," she said in a low voice, but every word was so sharp and indelible, that Daria must remember it forever. "I loved him so much. Someday you might understand that. I don't know how you found out. And I don't want to know. It's not in my power to understand such things. But I know I did right by you, Daria. Nobody can say differently. I thought—I thought I could keep you safe."

Slowly Daria stood up. It occurred to her that her mother was moving and speaking as in slow motion. Her breathing was heavy. Her skin seemed waxen, with the muscles soft and shrunken, as if all energy had been drained from her body.

For the first time in Daria's mind—in every part of her being—came the clear and certain awareness that her mother was a distinct and separate person.

"I happen to be her daughter," she said to herself, dazed, "but she is completely separate from me. We are like any two people. We can come together or grow far apart."

They did not look at each other, but in that moment Daria knew they stood at the balance. Another accusation, a sharp retort, and something would change between them forever. The rift would widen beyond mending. Only silence could save them now.

With a great sigh, Daria turned and went to her room.

10

*

The screech of tires. The wild, bucking motion of an automobile gone out of control. A high-pitched whine, like the distant whistle of a train bearing down upon her, and then came the grinding of metal against metal, the explosive shattering of glass, the single scream from the woman in the driver's seat.

Car crash. Car crash, with Peg slumped over the wheel, unconscious, bleeding from a deep gash in her forehead. And from the other car, slowly emerging, dazed but unhurt, came Daria herself.

She felt the same, familiar ache in her chest as she awakened. That dream. She had almost forgotten it; it had not reappeared for several years. Now, here it was again, and with it a new dread. It could be a premonition.

Daria lay awake, her body stiff. She thought of going out to the hall to get Priscilla. But she heard muffled sounds from the other side of the wall. Was it the sound of weeping? Daria lay stiff and still, unable to move.

As a small child, whenever she'd had this dream—the car crash dream—she would run into her mother's bed. They would lie close together, whispering. Mother would reach out, touch her forehead, give her a hug. "I love you, Mom!" Daria would exclaim.

"I love you, too, baby. So much." Then she would ask, "Was it the same old dream again?"

"Yes. Oh, don't ever go away and get killed, Mama!"

"I'll be very careful, honey."

What had happened to the two of them? Daria lay in her bed, imagining that she might go and tap at her mother's door, that they'd sit and talk . . . but no. It didn't work anymore. Whenever they got to talking, Peg would bring up something like Daria's math grades, or she'd begin to lecture about something she thought Daria ought to know, or she'd launch into explaining why Daria ought to start helping around the house more. Every time they started to really talk, it seemed that Peg tried to make Daria do something, to try to change her.

How could she change and still be herself? She was different from her mother. Why couldn't Peg understand and accept that? Why, for instance, couldn't she take pride in Daria's art and encourage her, as other mothers did? Whenever she saw Daria sketching, Peg only looked annoyed, tightening her lips; and even when she said nothing, Daria heard echoes of past lectures: "Don't spend so much time on this foolishness, Daria! Be practical. Unfortunately, the women in our family have always had to support themselves . . ."

How *had* Grandma supported herself and her two little girls? Daria knew that Grandpa had left them when Peg was only seven. For most of Peg's childhood it had been just Peg, her sister, Carola, and their mother. How had they managed?

It seemed suddenly vital to know, but now Daria dared not ask. Since that night, everything was changed. It had been over a week since Daria had said the words, "I am a bastard, and I guess that makes you a—"

If Peg's hand hadn't shot out, would she actually have said that word to her mother? Daria didn't know. She only knew that all tenderness between them was gone. The whole weekend, with Peg home from work, they had merely coexisted, hardly speaking; and to make matters worse, Rob hadn't been able to meet her after all. "Next Sunday," he had promised, leaving Daria alone with her books and her mother's silent anger.

Sometimes Daria caught her mother gazing at her intently, then quickly looking away. It was almost as if she suspected that something strange was happening. Then Daria recalled what her mother had said that night, "It's not in my power to understand such things . . ." It was a strange choice of words for a woman who scoffed at anything abstract or mysterious, and who despised anything that even hinted of the occult.

Often Peg seemed about to speak, to ask some question. Then she reconsidered, and they talked only of perfunctory things.

"We're having lamb chops for dinner, Daria."

"Oh, good. Did you see my pink sweater?"

"I guess it's in the hamper."

And now the dream had come again—the car crash dream. It came one night, and then a second. By Friday Daria was too tense and nervous even to try to make conversation with Peg.

"Daria, please be sure to lock up before you go to sleep. I'll be out late tonight. My friend, Bonnie, and I are going to the movies." It was a Friday evening.

Daria felt a sudden pang of fear. She did not want to be alone—not after having the dream two nights in a row. If it were a premonition . . . what must she do? Was it a sign to her, that she must save her mother?

Casually she asked, "Are you going far?"

"To the New Coast Theater—why?"

"That means you'll be driving."

"Well, of course."

"Can I come?"

Peg hesitated. "Oh, I don't think so. It's not the kind of movie you'd enjoy."

"You mean it's sexy?" Daria demanded.

Peg faced her, hands on hips, the red spots showing faintly on her throat. "I just don't think you'd enjoy the subject at all, Daria. It has nothing to do with sex. It happens to be a French film with subtitles, the kind you once said you'd never go to again if someone paid you a thousand dollars. Now, if you want to go to the show with me sometime, we'll plan it ahead and see something we'd both enjoy."

A huge, hard lump in Daria's throat spread throughout her chest, her whole body. She wanted to scream out her grief and fear. She wanted to beg her mother, "Don't go!" But something stronger even than loneliness and fear prevented her.

She turned away. "That's all right," she said coldly. "Actually, I was planning to spend the night with Nan McGraw. I really just wondered."

"Write down Nan's phone number then, in case I need to reach you."

"Why on earth would you want to reach me?" Daria cried out. "I don't want you to call me there. Mrs. Mc-Graw would think it was strange. Mrs. McGraw doesn't spy on Nan. She trusts her."

Daria waited for her mother's retort. It never came. Later, from her bedroom, Daria heard her mother calling, "Good-bye, Daria. I'm leaving two dollars on the kitchen table for you. In case you and Nan go to the movies or something. It's your allowance."

Daria sat on her bed stiffly, eyes wide, mouth resolutely firm. After a short silence she heard Peg's footsteps retreating. Then the door was closed with a sharp click.

Quickly Daria ran to the telephone and dialed Nan's number, silently praying that she would answer and invite Daria to stay over. Please, please, she begged, as the phone rang once, twice, and a third time. Please don't make me be alone tonight.

Nan answered, and immediately said, "Hey, Dari—I was going to call you. Can you stay over tonight?"

"Oh, yes!" Daria almost shouted with relief. "My mom's gone out. I'll walk over. Want to meet me half-way?"

"Sure. I'll leave right now. Meet you on Beach and Carmel."

They met and walked to Nan's, talking and laughing. Some boys went by in a car, whistling and hooting, and Daria and Nan started talking about the boys they knew at school.

"Well, everybody knows you're going with Rob Turner," Nan remarked.

"*Going* with him!" Daria exclaimed. "Who said?"

"You go around together, don't you?"

"Yes," Daria said slowly. "I guess I hadn't thought of it that way. We're friends."

"That's what's so terrific," Nan said. "You really *like* each other. Most people just go together because everybody thinks they'd make a cute couple. Like Kelly and Charlie Lacey—I don't think they know anything about each other, really."

Absentmindedly Daria nodded. It didn't seem so important now about Kelly and Charlie.

At Nan's house, a supper of baked ham was waiting, and Daria ate ravenously. Nan's father wasn't at all as she'd imagined; a sober scientist, preoccupied and distant. He laughed a great deal, listened intently when someone spoke, then waited several moments more, holding the person's gaze in case something more was to be added. That made it easy to talk to him. They sat at the table talking long after dessert was finished. At home, dinner

95

never lasted more than twenty minutes. Afterward, Peg always had something more important to do.

Daria had never seen Nan's room. On one wall were shelves, floor to ceiling, filled with books and plants. The green plants grew luxuriantly, their stems trailing down, with leaves large and full.

"What gorgeous plants!" Daria exclaimed. "Do you take care of them?"

"My mom taught me about plants," Nan said, beaming. "I've got nineteen of them."

"But they're all so—so healthy! When I get a plant it usually dies."

"Well, my mom talks to plants."

"You're kidding."

"No, really. She reads books about it." Nan grinned and sat down on the floor, hugging her knees. Daria sat down beside her.

Daria laughed. "You mean it makes a difference?"

"It really does."

"Weird," Daria said, and immediately she felt a pang of foreboding.

"I'll tell you something even more spooky." Nan stretched out flat on her stomach. "My mom can *always* find a parking place."

Daria looked at her quizzically.

"Whenever we go out, to the store or the show or anywhere, she always gets a parking place right in front of where we want to go."

"But, Nan, everybody finds parking places eventually."

"This is different," Nan insisted.

"Then she's lucky," Daria replied.

"No. It's uncanny. Even my dad says so."

"Do you mean that your mother *wishes* for a parking place and then gets her wish?"

"Oh, she doesn't do anything, consciously," Nan said.

"She hasn't any idea how it works. I guess she just thinks to herself that she wants to park the car now, and there's always a place. Maybe it's a form of psychokinesis. I've read about that . . . "

"So have I," Daria murmured with the uneasy sensation that things were going too far.

". . . the ability to influence matter."

Cautiously Daria asked, "Can your mother do anything—else?"

"Nope." Nan shook her head. "Just parking places. Dad thinks it's hilarious. Says she ought to be a taxi driver."

"Well, how does he explain it?"

"Oh, he doesn't. My dad says the first thing a good scientist admits is that science doesn't have all the answers."

"Want to do something?" Daria's uneasiness grew into a strange, prickling sensation. "Want to play Monopoly?"

"OK." Nan flung open her closet door and squatted down beside a large trunk filled with old clothes, toys and games.

Daria chuckled. "This looks like my closet."

"I hate to throw anything away," Nan admitted.

"Doesn't your mom yell?"

"Yeah, but she can't complain too much. You should see our garage. She saves everything, too." Nan groped under several boxes, took out a stack of coloring books and old school notebooks, reaching underneath for the games.

Daria, squatting beside her, gazed idly at the assortment. Her eyes focused on a thick white baby book with the gold lettered title, OUR BABY. Beneath those letters was an engraving in gold. The name—the name made her shudder.

"Nan . . ." It came out as a whisper. Still her eyes

97

were fixed hypnotically on the book with its gold letters, the baby's name especially engraved, MAUDE NANETTE MCGRAW.

"Who is Maude?" Daria's voice broke.

"Oh, that's me." Nan sat back on her heels. "Please don't tell anyone! My real name's Maude. Isn't it awful? So I go by my middle name Nanette, which really isn't me, either, so I shortened it to Nan. See, my dad's parents wanted me to have an Irish name, and they suggested Maude, after my great-great—"

"Irish? Are you Irish?"

"What of it! I'm part French, part Irish, and there's some German and Scottish, too."

They sat facing each other, Daria staring as if she were seeing Nan for the first time—the calm blue eyes and short brown hair, the frank, open expression on her freckled face. Suddenly Nan seemed different. She was a link to the mystery. Without doubt, she was a friend. But a friend chosen for her by whom? Or—by what?

"Nan." Daria's voice still shook. "There's something I've got to tell you."

"What's wrong, Daria? You look so strange."

Slowly, with great difficulty, Daria began to tell Nan about the voice, the vision in the dish, and the dream. It sounded preposterous even to her own ears. Daria stammered and twisted her hands, wishing desperately to find the right way to make Nan understand and believe her.

"Nobody had ever told me about my father, Nan," Daria continued her tale. "There's no way I could have known. And then in the dream She said, 'Tell Maude, the Irish one, the one who wears green.' "

"I'm not wearing green," Nan said.

Daria, close to tears, only shrugged and shook her head.

"Whatever it is," Nan said softly, "you've had a traumatic experience. I knew something had happened to you," she added. "You've been acting so—so different. I kept thinking about it. I asked Kelly and Sue and Claire, but they just said they didn't know, except that—well, somebody said you were maybe getting stuck-up. Because of Rob."

"Somebody," Daria muttered. Anger came in a swift flash. Kelly. For sure it was Kelly. Talking behind her back, trying to turn people against her. And why? To cover up for her own cowardice.

Anger made Daria's voice brusk as she asked Nan, "You won't tell the others?"

"Of course not." Nan was silent for a time. Then she said soberly, "Don't you think you should tell your mother about this, Daria?"

"No!"

"If it were me—" Nan began.

"My mother," Daria said sharply, "isn't like your mother. I can't tell anyone except Rob, and now you. And you don't really believe me." She felt helpless and cheated. She almost wanted to shake Nan, force her to believe. "Listen," she cried, "in the dream, She mentioned your real name. She knew it was Maude. Isn't that proof enough? And She even said you'd be open to new ideas, and now . . ."

"But that's ridiculous!" Nan cried. "You're trying to make me believe in Her by what She's supposed to have said. Don't you see how illogical? . . ."

Dully Daria persisted, "But that day at the library—you were so excited, so tuned in to this stuff . . ."

"And I am! I'm not saying these things aren't possible. But I . . ." Nan looked down at her hands, then she faced Daria squarely. "It was hard for you to believe about my mom's parking places," she said pointedly. "I'm not saying you're lying," she added quickly. "It's just so very

99

hard to understand. What if somebody told you these far-out things. I mean, it isn't as if you can prove it."

Daria slowly shook her head.

Nan turned away suddenly, made her tone brisk. "Look, maybe somebody is just working telepathy on you—you know, putting thoughts into your head through some psychic means."

"Like my mother?"

"Why not? It makes as much sense as any other theory. I've read about people sending telepathic messages."

"So have I, usually in time of danger." With a shudder, she remembered the car crash dream, and she told Nan about it, ending, "I didn't even want my mother to drive tonight."

"But, Dari," Nan argued, "dreams aren't really what they seem, are they? If you dream about a bear attacking you, the bear really stands for something else. It's a metaphor."

"Sounds like a disease," Daria said, grinning.

"It's a symbol," Nan persisted. "In your dream the car crash might symbolize something else. It might not even be your mother, either."

"Maybe," Daria said. "But what if it is a premonition? Like the time I knew my grandmother was dead?"

"You weren't dreaming that time," Nan pointed out.

"Well, maybe now something new is starting—premonitions in my dreams. How would I know? Just like the face in the dish was new, and everything else . . ."

"Well, if it's a premonition," Nan said, "then that's the purpose behind all these strange things, and you don't have to wonder anymore. Lots of people have premonitions."

"But, Nan," Daria cried, "that means my mother might die or get badly hurt!"

"But you said you've had these dreams before," Nan argued just as heatedly. "And your mom hasn't died."

"But how am I to know for sure, Nan? What I'm telling you is true. It's not something I'd wish for. It—it makes me feel like a freak."

"A freak!" Nan exclaimed, her eyes wide. "Dari, I'd give anything to have that kind of thing happen to me. I mean, to have something extra—a power—to know, really *know* what the world is all about, and what lies on the other side of . . ."

"But," Daria broke in softly, "nobody would believe you."

For a moment Nan was stunned into silence. Then she flushed.

"I see what you mean," she said. "I *want* to believe. Really, I do." She was nearly whispering with vexation. "But it's too incredible, even too fabulous . . ."

Daria said nothing more. Later, she didn't even mention her observation that Nan's pajamas and matching robe were a lovely shade of lime green.

11

*

On Sunday the sky over Marble Beach was the clearest blue imaginable. The ocean took on a rich royal blue; against it white sails in the distance floated gently by, scarcely seeming to move in the water.

A breeze blew to cool them as they lay on the sand. Rob had brought his large red beach towel. They lay on it together, facing the ocean, Daria absorbed by listening. Never before had a boy confided in her.

"I don't tell this to many people," Rob said, "for obvious reasons. You'll see what I mean." He sat up, arms wrapped around his knees, and while he spoke he looked out to sea.

"It started when I was in fifth grade," he began. "To me, the important thing was baseball. It was baseball season, and I was in the league, the pitcher. That was four years ago."

Daria turned, shielding her eyes, to look at him. "Four years ago? You're in eighth grade now . . . that would make it three years."

"I'm a grade behind," he said. "You'll soon know why. Well, that day I'd been at practice, and I was pitching great. I mean, I was really sharp for the season, and batting well after practicing with my dad all winter. I was walking home from practice. It was only half a mile or so to my house from the field. While I was walking—I don't know exactly how to describe it—I began to feel strange.

I got a tightness in my throat, and a terrible headache. And I felt so hot! My face felt as if it was burning, and my hands felt kind of numb.

"When I got home," Rob continued, "I started to vomit. My mom took one look at me and called the doctor. She said later my face was just beet red, and I was sweating and could hardly talk. She thought I'd gotten hurt playing ball. Well, the doctor came—he lived just a couple of blocks away, and it was a Saturday. He said I had to go to the hospital. And that was the last thing I remembered . . ."

"You passed out?" Daria asked.

"Listen. Next thing I knew I woke up one day in a hospital, in a room all alone. I was just lying there looking at the wall, trying to figure out how I'd gotten there, when a nurse came in. You never saw such a commotion. Other nurses came running in, and my doctor, and they called my parents right away. Everybody was so excited, but nobody would tell me anything until my parents got there. Then I found out why. Daria, I'd gone into the hospital one day in April. When I opened my eyes and looked around, it was August. I'd been in a coma all that time."

"Rob! My God . . ."

"I had a sickness called encephalitis," Rob said. "They told me later that they'd given me up. The coma was very deep, and the disease itself—it's an inflammation of the brain, you know. The doctors had been preparing my parents for my death. They'd also been preparing them to accept the fact that if I did pull through—although the chances were very slight—I'd probably have brain damage."

"But you woke up—cured?"

"Totally cured," Rob said, smiling, "and with no brain damage whatsoever. I've been tested several times."

103

"Does it happen very often that people recover from encephalitis?"

"I don't know the statistics," Rob said. "Most people don't come through the way I did, especially if they've been in a coma that long. It does happen sometimes, of course. And, depending upon what a person believes, they come to different conclusions."

Daria murmured, "I see. Some would call it a miracle, or. . . ."

"Doctors call it a reversal, they mention the will to live as being a factor. They can't fully explain it, either. What happened to me? I can't really say. Of course, I only know what my parents told me."

"But Rob, this isn't anything like my visions, or any psychic—"

"Well, wait till you hear the rest," Rob said. "To sum up, here the doctors were saying there was almost no hope that I'd live. My vital signs were getting weaker. Brain activity was very weak. My parents—you can imagine. I'm an only child. They were just desperate."

Rob moistened his lips, cleared his throat, and looked out to the ocean again, as if telling it were an effort.

"Does it bother you to talk about this?" Daria moved nearer, and Rob took her hand briefly.

"No, I want to tell you, Daria. I haven't told anybody. It's just so hard to explain, because what I'm going to tell you sounds so unscientific, and I've always been taught to question things."

Daria smiled. "I know."

"Now, my dad isn't the sort of person who just believes everything he hears. He's a psychologist. His whole training has been to study and observe and get information by scientific methods. Psychology isn't a science like chemistry or physics," Rob said, "but psychologists use scientific methods to study cause and effect."

Daria nodded.

"When the doctors said there was hardly any hope, my folks didn't know where to turn. I guess they just gave up. Then a strange thing happened. Now, you've got to know that my mother had never been involved in any sort of mysticism, either. But one day when she was driving to the hospital to see me, instead of listening to her classical music station the way she always does, she heard another station. What happened, she says, is that the tuning dial was stuck, and she couldn't get her music station. She was about to turn the radio off when she heard something that sort of grabbed her.

"It was one of those religious programs, but it was different. The woman was talking about healing through psychic power. The more she spoke, my mother said, the more she felt she had to stop the car and really listen and try to understand what this woman was talking about. Because she was saying that very often people who are in physical danger need not die, if only they got the right psychic information."

Rob paused briefly, catching his breath, and Daria urged him, "Go on!"

"My mother pulled off to the side of the road and just listened. Then, instead of going to the hospital, she drove straight to my father's office. She told him that she wanted to consult somebody who was a spiritual healer, and who might help me—psychically."

Rob sighed. "Now, you can imagine how, ordinarily, my dad would feel about an idea like that. But he was desperate by that time. So he did some research and found out about a psychic healer named Jethro Billings. Some of the stories about this Jethro Billings were pretty fantastic, but my dad asked himself, what did he have to lose? So he went to see this man, Jethro Billings, and told him about me. My parents drove to Dunover City, about forty miles east of here. They persuaded this Mr. Billings to come out to the hospital.''

''But were they convinced at that point that he could help?'' Daria asked.

''No. But they liked him and figured it couldn't hurt. So Mr. Billings came, and after sitting by my bed for about half an hour, he told my parents that mine was not a simple case. He said he was getting certain vibrations that made him know . . .'' Now Rob gave Daria a crooked smile and said, ''I don't think you're going to believe this.''

''Try me!''

''He said my sickness had to do with certain problems of mine that had occurred in—in my past lives.''

''Past lives!'' It was nearly a shriek, and Rob, laughing, shushed her.

''I warned you it would be hard to believe. I have trouble believing it myself. But it doesn't really matter, does it? I'm cured.''

''Well, how did it happen?''

''Jethro Billings stayed with me several hours, my folks said, just holding my hands. His eyes were closed part of the time, and other times they were open. At all times he seemed to be slightly removed. Not in a trance, exactly, but certainly meditating. After a while he told my parents that he had tuned in to my past lives, and that one in particular—the most recent one—was causing the problem.''

''You mean he said you'd lived before? That you've been *reincarnated*? And something back *then* was making you sick?''

''Yes,'' Rob said. He stood up, stretching.

Daria leaped to her feet. ''Aren't you going to tell me the rest?''

''Sure. I just thought we'd walk awhile. I'm getting stiff from sitting still so long.''

They began to walk, and Rob continued. "Jethro Billings said I had lived before in Denmark, and that I was born in the year 1785 to a couple who were poor farmers. We lived in a northern village, and I had four sisters and a brother, all younger than I. One day, when I was eleven, two of my sisters and my little brother and I went out to bring in firewood. We had a small wagon with us, and the weather was clear, although it had snowed the night before. We were warmly dressed, and we'd often gone out into the snow looking for wood.

"We went into the woods near a small lake, which was, naturally, frozen over. As we began to gather wood, I started a game with my brother and sisters. I said I'd shut my eyes and lean against a tree, and they were to gather all the wood they could and drop it into the cart behind me, and then run away again. I would guess, each time, how many pieces of wood they had collected. See, I was making a game of it, to get them to do all the work.

"The game continued. I was feeling happy and proud of myself for having tricked them into gathering all the wood. In their search they went farther and farther, always running back. Then they crossed the small lake, looking for more wood on the other side. They were running and shouting. The ice cracked, a deep and terrible hole. The three of them—all three of them—fell into the icy lake and were drowned."

Rob stopped, sitting down near the shore.

"And then?" Daria whispered, sitting down beside him.

"I went home at last, without my sisters and brother. Home to tell my parents what had happened, and then— then I lived the rest of my life in an agony of guilt that was almost unbearable. I died at the age of twenty-eight in that life, according to Jethro Billings. I died from being shot in a hunting accident."

"But, Rob," cried Daria, "even if such a thing were

remotely true, what would it have to do with getting encephalitis?''

''Well, Jethro Billings said that in my past life, as the Danish boy, after the age of ten my life was so totally unbearable that now, in *this* life, having reached the same age, I just couldn't cope. Also, I'd never gotten rid of that awful guilt. My present self—my *entity* or inner self—maybe thought I needed to die as punishment for what I'd done. Or else, it had the idea that once this body reached the age of ten, terrible suffering would follow. So, according to Jethro Billings, my inner self, or my subconscious mechanism, whatever you call it, decided that at the age of ten I must die.''

''Rob! Are you saying that a person chooses to be sick?''

''I'm not saying anything, only telling you what Jethro Billings said.''

''And there are *several* lives?''

''Many, many lives. For all of us,'' Rob said soberly.

For several moments they remained silent, Daria trying to conceal her sense of shock. Was she actually expected to believe that Rob had not only been reincarnated, but that a past life had influenced him this way? It was too far-out—and yet, wasn't her own experience also incredible? Yes, but this was not a childish game—you believe me, and I'll believe you. She had to learn more.

She asked him, ''What did Jethro Billings do to you?''

''First he explained to my parents about the past life. I don't know what they thought—probably that he was nuts. But, again, what did they have to lose? They pretended to believe him. All he wanted to do was to put his hands on my head. They figured no harm could come from that. So they told him to go ahead.

''He explained that he was going to communicate with me through the mind. Directly, from his mind to mine.

He put his left hand on my forehead, and his right hand on the back of my head. He sat there like that for about twenty minutes, absolutely silent, all the while communicating thoughts to me: that I need not fear getting older than ten years; that I must not suffer again for that old guilt; that this life could be good, that I had new talents and abilities and could be of service to others. I don't remember any of these communications. All I know is that the next morning I woke up from my coma, and I was cured.''

"Of course, you might have been cured anyhow,'' Daria said. "It could be that Billings made up the whole thing, just to claim credit in case there was a cure.''

"Of course!'' Rob agreed. "And even if by some power we can't understand, Jethro Billings is able to heal people . . .''

"I've read about things like that,'' Daria murmured. "It's like some people have a sort of energy, a positive force that lets them heal others.''

Rob nodded. "OK. I've told myself that even if Jethro Billings can heal, that doesn't necessarily mean his theories of reincarnation are true, does it?''

Daria took a deep breath. There was one question she had to ask Rob, crude as it might sound.

"Rob,'' she asked, "this Jethro Billings—how much money did he charge your folks for this cure?''

"That's the other thing,'' Rob said grimly. "You always think about fraud, and people conning you out of money with phoney cures. Jethro Billings didn't charge my folks a penny. In fact, he even refused to take money for his gasoline.''

"But would he take other clients if your dad sent them? For money?''

"No. He makes his living working at a hardware store. It's his policy never to take any money for what he calls his 'readings.' He says money doesn't mean a thing when you understand matters of the spirit.''

For a long while they sat staring at the endless motion of the waves. Daria felt the rhythm of the ocean influence her own breathing, her heartbeat, and she began to think of a great and endless universe with each separate creation, whether distant star or tiny spider, moving together in rhythm, never dying, never ending, but flowing and changing, all connected, all one.

It seemed idyllic and unreal, like a fairy tale. In another way it was frightening to think of being caught up by universal forces one could not control.

"Rob," she said, "if your life is already determined, aren't you just like a puppet or a robot? According to what Jethro Billings said, your life is all mapped out.''

"No," Rob replied. "He just told me what I could do, not what I would do. Actually, when you know all the things that are possible, you have more choices than before. Like ESP—it's just another sense, another way of finding out about the world. I think it would broaden your choices.''

Daria was silent for several moments, staring out to sea. Then she asked softly, "Then why do some people get ESP messages, and others not?''

Rob stood up, reaching out his hand. "That's the big question," he said.

Daria held Rob's hand tightly, marveling that he could be so calm and objective. Of course, he had help. His father helped him and tried to understand. That made all the difference.

12

*

Whatever the source of her visions, they were sending her information that was accurate and true. Such things, it seemed to Daria, would not happen without a purpose. In the dream-vision, She had told Daria about Maude, and urged Daria to challenge her mother. Both were probably meant to serve as proof of Her reality, Her power. If that was so, surely other, more urgent messages would follow. Perhaps other dream-visions would come to guide her.

But the angels in their silvery clothes, and the dream-Grandma did not appear. Only one dream recurred—the high-pitched whistle of a train, the screech of tires, the crunching, grinding of metal upon metal, and Peg slumped over the wheel like a broken doll.

Was it a warning? Was she, somehow, supposed to avert a car crash and her mother's death? Maybe this, then, was the reason for all the other occurrences, to warn her to prepare for catastrophe. If that was so, then it was only a cruelty, for she lay in bed, helpless.

If she had been brought in isolation onto this planet, dropped onto Earth from some distant star, she could not feel more alone. In books she had read of other people like herself—clairvoyants, they were called. Most of the famous ones were dead now; their lives had been spent, often, in constant searching and controversy. But who was like her now? Nobody she knew. She would always be different. Only Rob understood, but his belief in her stemmed from his own story, even more incredible than hers.

In truth, Rob's story made her uneasy. Not when they were together, of course, but afterward, when she thought about it.

What did Rob's story really prove? It only showed that there are lots of mysteries in the world. They weren't necessarily connected. One could believe in telepathy or clairvoyance and still deny reincarnation.

Talk about reincarnation made Daria feel almost panicked. She would stiffen, like Priscilla did when she braced herself for counterattack. *Nonsense!* her logical mind would object. *Does he really think I'll swallow this?*

But when they were together, with Rob's hand in hers or his arm around her, it was all so different. Then she felt ashamed of her doubts. Their steps matched perfectly as they walked along the strand, moving slowly in counterpoint to the crashing waves, walking and talking. When Rob spoke, everything suddenly seemed so plausible and natural.

"It's as if we live in a kind of bubble that's our known universe," Rob said softly, his voice soothing and mellow. "Sometimes, somehow, there's a crack in that bubble. We get insights into other dimensions, other realities."

Often Nan was with them. She knew something of Rob's story, and she would talk about other theories. "There's a part of the human brain that seems to be inactive. At least, scientists can't find out what it's used for. Maybe it's the seat of extrasensory perception. Maybe a million years from now we'll have evolved, and we'll all be using ESP."

"So, what'll I do in the meantime?" Daria had tried to sound humorous, but she failed. "I still dream of the car crash," she said softly. "What am I supposed to do?"

She had not really expected an answer.

* * *

It was the last week of school. No more homework was assigned. Everyone was bored and restless, eager for summer vacation to begin.

"Want to go to Polo Joe's?" Nan asked.

Daria shook her head. "I've only got a quarter."

"Just enough for the Ferris wheel!" Rob said happily, grabbing her hand. "Come on. Let's go. To celebrate summer."

"I hate that old thing," Nan objected.

"Come on, sissy," Rob and Daria coaxed. "It's the only decent way to start summer. We'll sit on either side of you."

They ran the rest of the way, giggling and pushing as if they were little kids. They watched as the last ride ended, and Nan looked up, pointing. "Look! There's Kelly Baxter and Charlie Lacey."

Kelly and Charlie were still laughing hysterically when their ride was over. As they brushed past Daria, Kelly glanced up for an instant, recognition and a flash of fear on her face; then she resumed laughing as if everything and everyone around them were too funny for words.

"Friendly," Nan muttered sarcastically as they climbed into the basket. Immediately Nan clutched the iron bar, and even before the wheel began to move she was screaming.

Up, up, then surging down, Nan screamed through the entire ride; and when it was over, she laughed even harder than Rob and Daria. But Daria's laughter stopped abruptly. For an instant she felt as if a cloud had passed over the sun, chilling her, while simultaneously she heard the sharp screech of automobile tires.

But Rob and Nan went right on talking and laughing.

Daria turned to them sharply. "Didn't you hear that?"

They turned in surprise. "What? What's wrong?"

"I—nothing." Daria shivered. "Guess I'll go home. It's getting cold."

Rob and Nan looked at each other, and Nan said quickly, "We'll walk with you, OK?"

"Sure." As they walked, the sun felt bright again, and Daria smiled, linking arms with Rob on one side of her and Nan on the other, and she began to sing a tune they all knew from the radio.

"Come on in for a while," she said gaily. "I've got some records. We could make popcorn. Want to?"

"Great!" they said.

Home, the living room seemed smaller than usual, and Daria began to feel that maybe she ought not to have invited them in. She shrugged off her doubts, turned on the phonograph, but things still seemed too stiff and formal. When the first few songs were over, Daria turned off the record, wondering why she felt suddenly so awkward.

Rob, for some reason, kept looking around the room, rapping his hand against the arm of the chair. And Nan, usually so talkative, had clammed up completely.

"What's wrong with you two?" Daria demanded. "Did I do something wrong? Want some popcorn?"

Slowly Rob said, "It's pretty cold in here. Don't you notice it?"

"No." Daria smiled nervously. "I was cold before. But—listen, it's nearly summer, and hot outside."

Nan began to walk around the room. "Daria," she said, "it really is cold."

"All right. Do you want me to make some hot chocolate?"

"No. That's OK," they said.

"Well, I'll go upstairs and check the windows," Daria said. "Sometimes if we leave a window open up there, it makes a terrible draft."

She went up quickly, checked her mother's room and

found the windows shut. Then in her own room—yes, the window was open and the curtains were blowing, the blind making small click, clicking sounds as it struck the window frame again and again. With a swift motion Daria slammed down the window. She turned to leave. But still the click, click, clicking of the blind continued. It became louder, louder, and with it a bone-piercing chill swept through the room.

She stood totally still, looked all around. Then she turned, but somehow she could not move, as if unseen hands held her rooted, and now the cold gave way to such a wind as might blow in the mountains on the sharpest winter night. But it was summer, summer, and with that thought Daria's mouth went dry and her heart began to pound in her ears.

The pounding enclosed her, the eerie cold gripped her hands. Then came the voice, stark and crisp but very commanding, and with it a shape that was white and wispy, like swirling snow, as if the form could scarcely be contained.

"Daria!" The voice was sharp and stern. "You are going to have a visitor. Listen! She is coming soon. You must greet her. You must go with her. Listen to the things she tells you. She has an important message . . ."

A sudden scream pierced the air. In that instant the icy coldness disappeared. The voice and the vision vanished. All was as before, except that Daria's legs felt spongy and weak, as if she had been climbing for hours. She turned and saw Nan standing in the doorway, hand uplifted, mouth still wide from her scream.

"Daria!" Rob came bounding up the stairs. "It's so cold in here! Nan, what happened?"

"Did you see it?" Daria whispered.

Nan's face was dead white, and her hand trembled as she pointed toward the window. "I—I felt it," Nan whispered. "I felt the cold and something else—like fog—clammy fog coming in—in through the window."

"Come on," Rob murmured, taking Nan's arm. "Let's go downstairs."

"Rob, did you see it?" Daria moved slowly, with effort, half leaning against Rob as they all started down the stairs.

"I didn't see it," Rob said grimly, "but I didn't have to. I'm convinced. I can see your face, and Nan's—the shock . . ."

"My God, Daria," Nan moaned. "I'm so sorry! I didn't know before. Oh, Daria, it's really . . ."

The front door was flung open. Midway down the stairs the three of them stopped as Peg confronted them, her face hard and accusing.

"Exactly what," she demanded, "is going on here? I come home an hour early, and what are you kids doing upstairs?" She was pale with anger, furious, even in her stance. "Daria, if you had any sense of propriety . . . I have told you countless times that before you have guests you're to check with me first."

"Mom, we only—"

"I don't like to embarrass you, children, but you will have to leave. *Now*. I will not allow Daria to have guests upstairs when I'm not home. Daria, you know better. I'm surprised at you."

"Mrs. Peterson!" Rob's voice was firm, though polite. "I think Daria isn't feeling well."

"Oh?" She peered at Rob. "So, what were you doing, taking care of her?"

"I'm OK, Rob," Daria said softly. "I'll talk to you later."

"No you won't," Peg Peterson snapped. "No telephone privileges for you tonight."

* * *

116

That night, after her mother had gone to sleep, Daria sat on the kitchen floor, cradling the telephone receiver in her hands. She debated with herself. Should she call him? She had never phoned a boy before. It was past ten. His folks might be mad.

Call him!

Better not.

I've got to talk to him!

The contest raged in her head, even while she was dialing his number, and while he answered in a low voice, "Hello."

"Oh, thank goodness. Are you still awake?"

"I never go to sleep." His voice was so cheerful that Daria smiled. "Hardly ever."

"Listen, about this afternoon—my mother . . ."

"It's OK, Daria. Forget it."

"I never had a chance to tell you what happened, what She said," Daria whispered. "It happened again, and it's true!"

"Take it easy, Daria. You sound all upset and shaky."

"I am! Rob, She said I'm going to have a visitor, and it's true! Now, Rob, no way could my subconscious ever have made up anything like this. It's my Aunt Carola and Uncle Don. From Missouri. Rob, I haven't seen them since I was a baby, except for when my Grandma died and we went back for the funeral. Even then, I just saw them for a few minutes. In all these years they've never even written."

There was silence on the other end of the line. "Heavy," Rob finally admitted.

"Tonight my mother told me she'd just gotten the mail and she read the letter outside, before coming into the apartment. Remember how she had the mail in her hand? Well, it really was a shock to her, which is partly why she was so mean to you and Nan . . ."

117

"A shock? Why would it be?"

"I told you, they *never* communicate. I guess they never really got along. My mom never talks about her sister. And when she told me they were coming, she was just furious. She kept telling me how it was rude and inconsiderate, and just like Carola to . . ."

"Hey, slow down," Rob said. "What's so rude?"

"They're driving out here from Missouri," Daria explained. "They mailed the letter the day they left, so my mother has no way of reaching them. They'll probably be here in a couple of days. I'm so scared!"

"Scared of your own aunt?"

"I know it doesn't make sense," Daria whispered. "I somehow feel that this is what it's all been leading up to."

"Wait a minute," Rob said coaxingly. "Just relax for a minute. You sound all uptight. I'm going to talk to my dad, ask him for advice, OK? Just stay there by the phone."

"All right, Rob. Hurry!" As if something were about to overtake her, she crouched down close against the kitchen wall. "I don't want this!" she cried inwardly. "Give it to someone who does, like Nan!" Her head was throbbing.

"Daria." Rob's voice came through, calm and soothing. "My dad suggested you have some warm milk. That will help you relax. Do you have a headache?"

"How did you know?"

"Take an aspirin with it," Rob directed. "Then, when you go to your room, my dad suggested you should—um—you should try something else. Stop worrying about what the vision really is or where She comes from. Approach Her like a real, living entity. Tell Her—"

"Rob, I feel weird talking to an empty room, to a—"

"Just listen! Tell it you got the message, that your aunt is coming, and that you'll listen to her, just as you were ordered to do. Say that a few times, until you feel sure it's been received.''

''Rob, this isn't quite like reaching someone on the telephone! Is your dad humoring me?''

''Of course not. I told you my dad's been doing experiments with these things. He says it doesn't matter exactly *what* your spirit is. What's important now is how you feel about it, how you might control it. Maybe ghosts are part of the unconscious mind. Maybe they're something outside of us. Either way, why not try to communicate with it?''

''All right, teacher,'' Daria said. ''Excuse me, while I go telegraph a ghost.''

''Now you're OK,'' Rob said with a sigh of relief. ''Sarcastic again. That's a good sign. Will you do what my dad said?''

''Yes, master. But what's the point?''

''The point,'' Rob said patiently, ''is to keep you from being scared to death again tonight. You've had enough for one day.''

''I'm with you.''

''If you could learn to control the appearances, you wouldn't get caught off guard all the time. That's what's upsetting you. And—'' he hesitated, ''you might want to see somebody. My dad suggested it, somebody who's had experience with things like this. To help you adjust.''

''You mean a shrink?'' Her fear was gone now, and she could manage a grin. ''Rob, are you drumming up business for your dad?''

''Of course not!'' Rob exclaimed. ''My dad would be glad to talk to you, without charge, of course, if you wanted to. It would give you a different perspective.''

''I'll think about it.''

''He's been doing some lab experiments. You'd make a good subject for him,'' he said.

"I'll really think about it," she said softly. "But now, I'll fix milk and take aspirin and make contact with the spirit world."

"Good girl."

She whispered, "Good night, Rob."

He answered, "Good night, luv."

Later, although she felt self-conscious and slightly ridiculous, she whispered into the silence of her room, "Grandma! You were right. Aunt Carola is coming. I received your message. I will listen to her. I'll do what you said." She paused, then added, "Let me rest now, please."

Daria got into bed. For the first time in months or even years, she remembered a simple, childish prayer. Was it wrong, she wondered, wrong before God to delve into such mysteries?

She remembered, from some hazy past, a Bible verse told to her from one of the endless procession of babysitters. "Regard not them that have familiar spirits."

Familiar spirits. Regard not them. "Oh, God," she prayed silently, "forgive me if it is really wrong. But I must know. I must dare to find out."

Regard not them. Familiar spirits. . . .

Daria lay still, breathing deeply, murmuring the words in her mind. As she drifted very near sleep, there came the fragrance. It was not the strong, heady scent of prior nights. The same fragrance emerged now in gentle, subtle form, tamed into a delicate, pleasing scent that made her feel secure.

13

*

The first few days of summer vacation were disappointing. The hours seemed to drag. It was usually so. The long-awaited time, once arrived, could not quite measure up to the expectation.

Daria felt restless and uneasy. She had signed up for three summer school classes—art, typing, and practical nursing. Classes would begin in two weeks, but Daria still felt undecided about her program.

The art teacher, a Miss Antoinette Morehead, had been hired especially as a visiting artist, just for the summer. Twenty-five students had been chosen to work with her, Daria among them. If Miss Morehead approved, a few students could work with her for all three periods. Daria simply couldn't decide what to do. She longed to work with a real artist. At the same time she felt shy and unprepared, uncertain of what seemed the right choice. And it would cause a hassle with her mother.

Perhaps She would reveal it. But no further messages came. Perhaps Carola's visit would settle something; She had told Daria of its importance. But several days went by, past the time it would normally take to drive from Missouri to California.

Daria repeatedly asked her mother how long it might take.

Peg seemed unconcerned. "Three or four days," she said. "Maybe five."

"It's been more than five!" Daria exclaimed.

Three more days passed. Daria's restlessness turned to anxiety, and all her fears were concentrated on one idea. The dream of the car crash. Suppose the dream of the car crash had been a real premonition. And suppose the woman she had seen slumped over the wheel was not her mother, but her aunt. It could be. No doubt, as sisters, they looked something alike.

Whenever the telephone or the doorbell rang, Daria braced herself, took two deep breaths and ran, gulping, to answer.

"Hi! You look as if you've seen a ghost!" It was Rob at the door, grinning.

"Very funny." Daria made a face at him, then grinned back, leading him inside.

"The car crash again?" he asked.

Daria nodded. "Rob, do you think the time will ever come when we discuss the usual things? I mean, like other people do?"

He smiled good-naturedly, shaking his head. "How dull that would be." Soberly he added, "No word from your aunt, I guess."

"No." Daria shrugged. "Let's forget it. Want to walk over to the mini-park?"

"Sure. Got some old bread? We can feed the ducks."

Hand in hand they walked toward the miniature park, no larger than an ordinary lot—a small patch of greenery with several benches, a few shade trees and a tiny pond where half a dozen or so ducks lived.

"It's so pretty here," Daria said softly, when the ducks had been fed and she and Rob sat down on the lawn. "I wish . . ."

"That none of it had happened?" Rob asked.

"No. I just wish I could always feel the way I do now. Not upset or confused—just OK. Very OK."

"I've got an idea," Rob said, "if you want to try it."

"About my visions?"

He nodded. "You could try to control the appearances. If you got relaxed—maybe you could make Her—it—appear. Then you could ask Her questions. It wouldn't scare you so much, because *you* could decide. You'd be in control."

Daria nodded. "Might be worth a try." Her tone was casual, but her heart began to race at the enormity of the idea. "If I were alone, controlled my state of mind and asked Her to come . . ."

"You could talk to Her then, get Her to answer some of your questions. After all, a spirit should know more about psychic matters than you or I."

"Rob, I can't figure you out. Are you joking?"

"Only partly," he said, laughing. "This—this ghost *is* real. My dad says it depends on your definition of reality. Isn't the subconscious mind real? Isn't a dream real to the dreamer?"

"But we're talking about a reality that can throw a dish across the room," Daria said grimly. "Does your dad think that energy is coming from inside of me or from something outside?"

Rob shrugged. "Well, of course, that's the big question. Maybe if you did work with my dad—took some of those ESP tests, you could find out. At least you could make a start."

"Would you be there too?"

"Yes, if you want."

"And I'd just take tests? Like trying to guess symbols on hidden cards and things like that?"

"Yes. Of course, you'd need your mother's permission. My dad won't work with any minors unless they have parents' approval."

"Oh-ho! Fat chance. I'd sooner get my ghost to appear

every time I snap my fingers, than even hint at ESP to my mother!"

At home, Daria's mother was already there, white-lipped, tense, and smoking.

"Mom!" Daria cried. "What's wrong? Mom, you *quit*, and now . . ." Daria saw the old familiar gestures, the pacing, inhaling, exhaling the swirling clouds of smoke. Her mother had quit eight months ago. Eight months of effort—ruined.

"I don't want to hear one word about smoking, Daria," her mother said warningly. "I mean it! It's *my* life and *my* body, and . . ." Suddenly she crushed out the cigarette, then ran to her purse, took out the pack and flung it at Daria.

"Take these!" she shouted. "Tear them up and throw them in the garbage. Oh, God, I think I'm going to be sick. How'd I ever get used to these in the first place?"

She shuddered, clutched her stomach, and suddenly she was laughing and weeping all at the same time. Calm again, she sat down on the sofa and said, "I'm sorry, Daria. I just sort of flipped out, as you'd say. I went out and bought those, and *I don't want them!* Carola's coming. She smokes incessantly. But what that's got to do with it, I don't know. I'm just upset. She's always made me feel like—well, like a little sister."

"Isn't that what you are?" Daria said.

"We're only three years apart. It's just that I—that she and my mother were always—well, that's water under the bridge. I can handle it," Peg said, chin high. "They're coming at seven. She called me at the bank. Can you beat that? She remembered where I work and called me there. They're coming for dinner. What'll we have? Should I send out for Chinese?"

124

"I think better not," Daria said. "They might not be used to it."

"You're right. A chicken, then. Do you think chicken?"

"Perfect. You could make biscuits, and I'll make my chocolate mousse for dessert."

"Oh, yes, honey, yes. Let's hurry and go to the store. We'll shop together."

It was the way it used to be. Years ago, they had rushed off to the shops together nearly every day, sometimes taking time to browse. They both loved to browse through the hardware store, envisioning jewelry and knickknacks they might create out of bolts and screws and wires, if they ever had time for such things. Someday, Peg would say, someday they'd buy a pile of stuff and play with it for hours on the kitchen table, maybe make jewelry and little sculptures and sell them at the community art festival that was held on the pier each summer.

They shopped quickly. For the first time in many months they worked side by side in the kitchen, Daria whipping up the egg whites for the mousse, Peg frying the chicken to a golden turn. Biscuits and fresh summer corn were added. They spoke very little, but there was an ease about their movements. After a time Daria said, "Summer school starts next week. I'm taking a full program."

"That's good. Summer can get pretty boring after a while."

"I'm taking typing and art," Daria said, "and home nursing."

"I didn't know you were interested in that."

"I didn't either," Daria said. "At least, I don't think I am."

"But you signed up for it."

"I thought it would be practical to know. I mean, I should know about first aid, and if I learn to type, maybe

I can get a job next summer. Well, I guess that's a stupid idea . . ."

"Not at all. It's a good idea. But since you love art so much . . ."

The doorbell rang, and suddenly the apartment seemed too small to contain the exuberant emotions that filled the air—the exclamations, laughter, the booming voice of Uncle Don, the high-pitched twitter of Aunt Carola, the gleam of her brassy blond hair, the golden tan of her long legs, ending in three inch high wedgies. . . . It was so sudden and unexpected that Daria shrank back, pressed against the wall in an awkward pose, as if she didn't live here, but were a stranger at a blaring, boisterous party.

She stood thus, waiting for them to notice her, yet wishing they wouldn't. They did, of course. Uncle Don spotted her and boomed out, "Good heavens, could this be Daria? I don't believe it. Look at this, Carola! Would you believe it? Peg, the kid's gorgeous. Isn't she gorgeous? Peg, what do you feed her? Sure grow tall in California—all that vitamin D. How old is she now? Fourteen? Fifteen?"

"Honey, it's so good to see you!" Aunt Carola's arms were around Daria, and she could smell a flower sweetness clinging to her aunt—a cologne splashed on liberally. Aunt Carola's embrace was light and cool, but lingering.

It took about fifteen minutes until they were all settled down in the living room. Peg served small glasses of sherry. Then Uncle Don, sitting in the large armchair, patted his hands down on the armrests several times, gazing around the room like a lord surveying his domain, nodded and murmured, "Very nice, Peg. Very comfortable." Then formally he launched the visit with the inquiry, "So, what's new?"

To Daria it was all so absurd, so meaningless—and yet so wonderful. Wonderful—to have family, an aunt and uncle coming to dinner, asking questions in that bold and forthright way, questions that only family had a right to ask, and did.

"How are you doing at school, Daria? Do you have a boyfriend, Daria?" Uncle Don's voice was lower now after dinner, his body more relaxed. He had complimented everything and enjoyed it immensely. Daria had almost forgotten how it might be to have a man sitting at the table and eating with a man's marvelous appetite.

"I—yes," Daria said, surprised at her own readiness to talk. "His name is Rob. We were in the same English class at school."

"Do you go out together?" Uncle Don watched Daria closely.

"Well, we go to the beach or for walks. We go to Polo Joe's for hamburgers. We don't have dates, exactly, I guess. We've never gone to the show or anything like that."

"Is he a gentleman?"

Daria flushed slightly, then met Uncle Don's gaze. "Yes."

"He is very nice," Peg said unexpectedly. "He came to visit Daria when she was sick. He's always polite to me on the phone."

"It's nice to have a boyfriend like that," Uncle Don said, beaming.

By eleven at night everything had been asked and answered, and Carola and Peg had shared a few old memories. But it seemed to Daria that the two sisters approached their past with wariness.

"Do you remember old Mrs. Ames?" Carola had asked. "Well, she died last year. And that Freddie Dickinson—you wouldn't believe it, he ran for mayor and won. Yes, Freddie! And, wait till I tell you who's already divorced three times . . ."

At last Uncle Don stood up and announced that it was time to go.

"How long are you staying in town?" Peg asked. "Will we see you again?"

"We're leaving tomorrow, right after checkout time at the motel," said Uncle Don. "Guess we'll just snoop around town till then."

"If I'd have known when you were coming," Peg said, "I would have planned to take the day off."

"That's all right, Peg. Listen, we come breezing in once in a blue moon, how could you be expected to know? Listen, you go on with your work. It's a fine job. It's been a grand evening. Just wonderful."

"Just wonderful," Aunt Carola echoed with a bright smile for Daria. "I loved your chocolate mousse. Would you send me the recipe?"

"Sure. Sure I will," Daria said, knowing that she never would, that Aunt Carola would never write—just as she knew that for some reason, she would surely be seeing Carola again before they left.

Daria had expected it. At nine the next morning, after Peg had left for work, the telephone rang. Aunt Carola on the other end of the line chattered in her breathless way.

"Oh, honey, I hope I didn't wake you, but I did want to catch you in case you were going out or something. Daria, I'd love to spend some time with you this morning. Don's going to get a haircut, and he said he wants to go down to the pier and maybe try some fishing, and I just hate that fishy smell and all, so I told him I'd meet him back at the motel at two, and meanwhile you and me could just spend some time together, maybe shopping, or lying on the beach or whatever you want. What do you think? Want to do it?"

128

Steady, Daria told herself. This is it. "Well, Aunt Carola, I . . ."

"Wouldn't you like to?" There was a wistful, almost sad quality in Carola's voice. "Wouldn't it be fun?"

"Yes, it would be fun," Daria said. "Yes, I'd love to be with you, Aunt Carola. I'll be ready whenever you say."

14

*

During that whole long morning with Aunt Carola, Daria felt almost as if she were seeing what they were doing through a haze. She was there, inside the picture. But she was also on the outside looking in, watching Carola and Daria, the two of them so very different, walking along the paths at the Botanical Gardens, sitting down in accord, talking greedily, eagerly, to make up for those many years.

Carola had expressed her great love for flowers. Daria led the way to the Botanical Gardens. She had not walked there in many years. Now the gardens were expanded. A fern grotto offered a lush, cool space of greenery, interspersed with large rocks. Further, Japanese bamboo and jasmine surrounded a covered wooden bridge. Beneath it a stream twisted and turned, leading to the grove of miniature fruit trees, then to the vast fields of asters, marigolds and snapdragons, and finally to the treasured formal rose garden.

Carola exclaimed over everything. To Daria, the brilliant colors and combined scents were almost overpowering. They returned to the fern grotto, to sit among the tall, lacy leaves. Only a few elderly people strolled along the paths. Gradually the silence and solitude worked its charm. Daria began to feel that part of her was here, breathing the greenery, feeling the cool thick grass beneath her— part of her hovered above it all, waiting.

Never before had anybody told Daria about her mother's

childhood. Peg's answers to such questions were always curt. "I don't remember," or, "It was so long ago—what's the difference? Everything changes."

But Carola seemed to savor her memories, recalling small details that anyone else might consider irrelevant. To Daria, they were fascinating.

"Peg was always the practical one, even when we were little kids. I remember she used to cook from the time she was only five. She'd make pancakes for Mama and me— can you imagine? My dad ran off, you know, and left us."

"Why did he?" Daria asked. Her voice was low, to match the soft, cool greenery.

"He was a nice man, Daria, and a good daddy. But he was also a drunkard. He didn't get mean when he drank, like some men do. But he got silly and shiftless. He'd spend every cent we had and just go horsing around. It got so my mother couldn't take it anymore. I mean, she had me and Peggy to think about, and my dad had us deep in debt. Pretty soon they wouldn't even give her credit at the corner drugstore."

"So your mother divorced him?"

"Oh, no. He just went off one day, and my mom didn't bother to find him. That is, she made up her mind it was better that way. She did love him. Peg was too little to know, but I saw her crying for him sometimes. She'd be standing by the parlor window in the dark, lookin' out, crying. It would be in the night when she thought we were asleep. My mother," she said proudly, "never cried in front of anybody. She was strong. She took care of herself and us. She never went around telling us how hard it was to take care of two little girls all by herself. I never did realize it, either, until I grew up and saw other people with their kids. I—Don and me can't have any kids of our own. We always thought about adopting, but you know how it is. Time goes by, and you neglect to do things.

131

Pretty soon you wake up one day and it's too late. I mean, I'm thirty-six years old. I guess I could still get a kid, but," she shrugged, "I don't know. It just seems like too much of a hassle, and you get set in your ways at my age."

"What was she like?" Daria asked. "Your mother . . ." The green of the grotto seemed like a soothing, fragrant veil of pale green touched with specks of silvery light. Daria sat back, her eyes half-closed, inhaling deeply.

"She was—how can I say? I loved her, my old lady. I guess I loved her more 'n I ever loved anybody. She wasn't very tall nor very short. Just average, I guess you'd say. She had light brown hair, until it turned to gray, of course, and very bright blue eyes. Hey, you've got blue eyes, ain't you? Well, hers were brighter, though. Sometimes you'd think they were like the eyes of a bird and could look right through you. Like, she always knew what Peg and me were up to. She always knew."

"Did you two do pranks and things?"

"Oh, sure." Carola nodded vehemently, taking a piece of chewing gum, offering one to Daria, who shook her head. "I quit smokin', you know," Carola said, "about three years ago. Chew this junk all the time now. Rots your teeth, you know, but what's a tooth compared to a lung?" She laughed heartily, her bosom heaving. "Like I said, my mother would know things about us. I remember one time I'd been playing in a big old tree down by the creek. I fell out of the tree and broke my arm. I was laying there on the ground, just crying. The other kids I was with all ran away, 'cause they were so scared they'd be blamed. See, we'd tied a rope around a limb, and it broke. Anyhow, suddenly there was my mother, running over like fury, as if she'd known exactly where to find me and what had happened. Our house was about two miles away, and there was no way she could have heard a thing. None of the other kids went to get her, either. I asked them all

132

afterward. Anyhow, there she was, and she picked me up and carried me, running, all the way to the doctor's. You'd think she would have collapsed, 'cause I was all of ten years old by then, and not skinny either. She carried me all the way. The doctor said my arm was broke real bad. He said if I had walked, causing it to move, the bone would have gone right through the skin. Oh, we played some pranks, we did, but we never went swinging from that tree again.''

"Tell me about the pranks," Daria said. She plucked out several leaves of grass and nibbled at the tender roots.

"Oh, as I said, your mother was always pretty good and didn't get into much mischief. I guess that's why it came as such a shock to us when she started up with Tracy Peterson. I mean, he wasn't from around our town, or anything, but just buzzed in one day from God knows where, and Peg just lost all her sense, it seemed like.''

"My father," Daria murmured. "Tell me, how did he look?''

"Oh, he was good-looking. Thin, sort of, but he had a good, wide mouth and a nice chin. I like a nice, strong chin. His didn't have a dimple, like Don's, but it was a good chin, and he had nice teeth. I think good teeth are very important. His eyes were gray, and his hair was a light, sandy color. In the summer it got very blond.''

"Was he strong? Was he tall? Did he have good muscles?'' At once the yearning flooded into Daria's being. If she could only know, only see him for just a moment, all would be resolved. Father! If he could take her hand, hold her in his arms, smile down at her—*be her father*. Did he love her? Would he have loved her if he'd have been here?

But he was dead, dead. He had always been dead, from the very moment of her birth. He had already been buried. Daria spit out the bits of grass. She pressed her lips tightly together.

"He was strong," Carola said. "I remember, he'd play four sets of tennis in an afternoon. Four sets, and in the blazing heat. And he loved to row. He could row for hours . . ."

"My mother told me that . . ."

"Peg had never been in love before. When she fell, wow, she fell hard. And nothing anybody could say would get through to her. Oh, no. Not Peg Whittlesey. So, when my mom told her time and again, 'Peg, he's just not for you,' of course, she wouldn't listen. I even told her. He just wasn't right for her. I mean, he was from Pittsburgh, and his whole upbringing . . . what could I say to her? She sure wasn't going to listen to me."

"But what was wrong with him?" Daria cried.

"Nothing!" Carola exclaimed vehemently, and her cheeks grew flushed with emotion. "He was great and handsome and strong and fine—but Daria, listen honey, he just wasn't for her. Don't you see? I guess you don't, living here in California. It's all so different. See, we lived in a small town. Folks don't take easily to strangers, especially men from the city. City slickers, they called 'em.

"Tracy was—well, he wasn't working steady. He'd put in a couple of weeks at the saw mill, and then he quit. People called him a drifter. Why he came to our town, I'm not sure. I think he was just driving through on his way west and stopped 'cause he ran out of funds. That shows you how different they were. Peg would never let that happen. Yeah, they were really just about opposites, her and Tracy."

She paused, nodding thoughtfully. "We all figured Peg would choose a local fellow, or someone she met at college. Somebody steady and reliable, who had a real job and wanted a house and kids—a family life. It was what Peg wanted, and Lord knows, what she needed, but she just went and got . . ."

"Got pregnant," Daria said. The words had slipped out so easily. "Got pregnant with me and never did marry him."

Carola drew back, amazed. "You know? She told you?"

"I just know it," Daria said evasively. "It doesn't matter now."

"No. She's done a good job of taking care of you."

Carola's face became even more vivid in color now, and she looked down at the grass under her feet. "Your mother changed her name to Peterson after he died. It wasn't so much wanting to be married as just taking a new name, just the way she started a new life, alone with you. I—I had advised her to—to give you away for adoption."

Daria stared down at her aunt's feet clad in the high wedgies, and she felt no emotion, only the faint chill of a sudden breeze.

"Your mom wouldn't hear of it. Said she wanted the baby and meant to keep it. Said she'd love it. I guess I gave her the wrong advice. I—I'm glad she kept you. And she's glad, of course."

"Is she?" Daria said. Then she asked, "Would he have married her, do you think, if he'd have come back?"

Carola shrugged. "I really don't know. He died when she was four months pregnant. He never knew about you. She wouldn't tell him. Didn't want to hold a man that way, she said. Peg's very independent. Always was. That's why she wouldn't listen when Mama warned her, and of course, Mama could tell what would happen, just as if it had been written in the evening news. She told Peg from the start, and many's the night I heard them arguing. 'Peggy,' my mother said, 'Peggy, darlin', don't get your heart set on this man. I beg you. It will come to naught.' That's how she talked, you know. The Irish in her. 'It will come to naught, for I see it ahead, clear as can be. Only

135

unhappiness for you with this man. He will leave you, child, and beyond his leaving, I see a cloud of black—' "

"What?" Daria cried, as if suddenly awakened out of a stupor. "What do you mean? What was she saying?"

Daria sat up, beginning to shiver. She wrapped her arms tightly around her bent knees, as if to keep warm, and still she urged Carola, "What are you saying? Are you saying that my grandmother *knew* he'd die? And she knew he'd leave her first? How could she have known?"

Carola's eyebrows shot up, and she drew back, as if to see Daria more clearly. "But Daria, didn't you know? Didn't your mom ever tell you? Our mother—your grandmother—was Rose Whittlesey. You mean she never told you? Rose Whittlesey was known all over Missouri and far beyond. I believe she's even mentioned in some books. She was a very gifted psychic. She was a medium."

All the rest of the day, after Carola had left her, Daria felt as if she were surrounded by a bubble of light. It was a soothing, varicolored haze of pink, yellow, green and blue. The hues shifted and changed as she recalled each word Carola had said, and added to the words certain other inflections and realizations.

Grandma. Of course. Grandma was a psychic and she, Daria, had received the gift.

Dubious gift, to make her different, to cause her fear . . . and yet she exalted! That spirit of her grandma, if it did still live somewhere in another realm, would never harm her. There was only love.

Home, Daria mechanically tended to tasks she usually hated. She ironed a stack of clothes, took several baskets-ful of laundry down to the washing machine. She dusted the furniture, all of it soothing and effortless, as she now thought of her possessions.

Oh, such possessions—a father she had never known, and who might not have even wanted her; but now she knew how well, how wildly he had been loved. A mother who wanted her so much—perhaps even more than other mothers—for to keep her meant such sacrifice. Now, too, she had a family, a real aunt and uncle who could link the past with the present for her. Her grandmother had been somebody important. Her grandmother had bequeathed her something. For all of them, for this strange and distant family, now there was only love.

Rose Whittlesey. Ah, the name had a lovely ring to it, now that she knew. Rose Whittlesey, psychic and medium, well-known in Missouri. Could it be that people still spoke of Rose Whittlesey and what she had done? Perhaps someday it would be possible to find out. Had she truly helped people?

Carola had said, "She helped people, my mother did. That is how she made her living and supported Peg and me. By giving readings."

"You mean she got paid for it? Like a fortune teller? Like that Madame Minerva down at the carnival?" For a moment Daria had hovered between excitement and disgust. Her grandmother . . . one of *those*!

"Of course not." Carola tossed her head and chewed vigorously on her gum. "It's really nothing like that. When your own mother's a psychic, you get used to it, and you know the difference between a real one and a fake. Mama used to have readings in our living room. Usually there'd be four or five people there, and she'd just slip into a trance as easily as people sip a glass of tea.

"Matter of fact," Carola said with a giggle, "often as not she would be sipping tea while she gave her readings. She said it kept her in touch with this sphere, you know, kept her from totally fading away. I don't know. I think she just liked her tea. Sometimes she'd pour in a tiny nip of brandy."

Carola giggled again. "It never harmed her. She was

137

the most sober lady I ever knew, but also she had a sense of humor. She said—what did she used to say? You mustn't ever lose your sense of humor when you get into important things. Because if something's important enough to really concern you, you mustn't let it swallow you up, but keep your focus. That is what laughter is for.''

Daria nodded slowly.

''Lots of people don't believe in psychics,'' said Carola, pulling out another piece of gum, discarding the first one in the bushes. ''It's easy to say you don't believe in something when you've never seen it. Well, I've seen all that stuff since I was little. I saw ectoplasm once.''

''You—saw it?''

''Yeah. Sure did. Came right down from the chimney, out of the fireplace, crept around a big lamp we had.''

''Weren't you scared?''

''No,'' Carola said simply. ''My mother was there. Why would I be scared? It just seemed like the most natural thing. I just accepted it.''

''But my mother didn't,'' Daria stated, beginning to understand the conflict that must have dominated their lives for years in that household in Missouri.

''Say—you're perceptive, you know? Yeah, Peg hated those readings. She hated it if kids found out what Mama did. Mama never would have charged money for it if she hadn't needed it for us. She hated taking money. So, she'd just leave an old shoebox there on the windowsill, and people would put in donations. We lived off that. Peg—practical Peg—she was the one who'd count the money after every sitting. They called it a 'circle'.''

''But how did Grandma help people?''

''By what she did,'' Carola said. ''Afterward, of course, she'd never know what she'd said while she was in the trance. But she'd get messages from the Other Side, you know. Mostly they were for people who'd lost their loved ones. Mama would sometimes be able to contact them. Or if she couldn't contact them directly, she'd get a message. And those spirits would usually say they were OK, and that they were happy over there. Sometimes they'd give advice to their relatives. Sometimes it really saved their lives.''

''Like how?''

''Like one man, his name was Mr. McCurdy. I remember he and his wife—a real skinny, sick-looking little thing—they came to the circle for a few months. One time Mama got a message from Mr. McCurdy's sister. She was in her trance, of course, and she said in that different voice, 'There is a message to Eddie.' That was Mr. McCurdy's first name. 'Eddie,' she said, 'you'd better get that balcony fixed. The underpinnings is rotting out. You'd better get it fixed.'

''Well, Mr. McCurdy did poke around the support beams for that balcony, but he couldn't see anything wrong. The next week he gets the same message, only more urgent. 'Eddie, please get that balcony fixed. If you don't, you're going to have a terrible accident.'

''So Mrs. McCurdy called out a building inspector, 'cause it really scared her, and sure enough, the man said those posts were so rotted under the ground, they were like to collapse any time, and of course the whole balcony would have come crashing down. If Mr. or Mrs. McCurdy had been standing on it, they'd have been killed.''

''But then if Grandma helped people,'' Daria asked, ''why was my mother so against it?''

''Oh, Peggy was just always afraid of what people might think. See, we're different, Peg and me. I don't care so much. Like, I know I'm too fat, and sometimes I look a mess, but I don't *care*. I can sort of move along easy, and things like that don't matter to me so much. Just like this old car we drive. But take Peggy. She'd work her tail off

139

to buy a respectable looking car where the door handles aren't always falling off. Peg always wanted to get on in the world. She's smart. Smarter than me, I guess. She always did good in school, and she wanted to go to college.''

"She did go. And to night school after that."

Carola nodded. "I know. That's what I mean. Peg always cared a whole lot about bettering herself. Always kept her clothes looking just so. I guess Mama and I embarrassed her a lot. I mean, you know how it is when kids find out your mother's holding seances in your house. Peg wouldn't ever let any of her friends come over."

"But after she grew up, what difference would it make about Grandma?"

"Well, after Peg got out of high school, she got a job and started going to college, too. It was hard for her, but she was doing it, and things *were* better between her and Mama. But then, of course, when Mama told her about Tracy . . ."

"She didn't believe it?"

"She couldn't believe it," Carola said. "Don't you see, Daria? She loved Tracy. Besides, if Peg had broken off with him because of what Mama predicted, that would have been admitting that she did have a special power. And Peg had always fought against that, all her life. She never could accept it."

"But she saw what your mom was doing!" Daria cried.

"Do people always believe what they see?" Carola asked. "No—Peg hated it, and it scared her something terrible. And you know why she was so scared? I think, inside herself, Peggy was more convinced than anybody of Mama's special power. I think that's why Peg was so dead set against it. Because somehow she thought Mama would use it to run her life, or that Mama would *make* things happen. And Peg was too spunky and independent

140

and practical for that. So, when she met Tracy, it was like a test, don't you see? She couldn't hear anything against him—wouldn't listen. Sometimes I think she fell in love all the harder, because we were all against it. Not that Tracy wasn't a terrific guy,'' Carola added quickly.

There was so much more Daria had wanted to hear from Carola. Too soon Carola had had to drive Daria back to the apartment. She and Don were bound for Oregon, to spend several weeks camping. For a moment as they said good-bye, Daria had the thought that Carola would invite her to join them. But the moment passed and nothing more was said, only a quick good-bye and a hasty kiss, and Carola saying, ''We'll meet again, Daria. We'll visit.''

''Great,'' Daria said, doubting it.

''I wish I'd have brought you a present, kid. I'll send you something from Oregon. I should have brought a present . . .''

''You did, Aunt Carola,'' Daria said. ''You did.''

15

*

Late in the afternoon Rob telephoned. "How about going to the show tonight?"

"Not tonight," Daria said. "I've got to tell you about today—this unbelievable day. But not yet. I sort of have to think about it by myself."

"I understand," Rob said softly.

"I know you do," Daria replied gratefully. "Listen, tonight I'm going to try . . ."

The door swung open and Peg entered, shoes in hand.

"I've got to go, Rob. My mom just came home."

"You're going to try—the contact?"

"Yes."

"Let me know what happens. You can phone me, even if it's late."

"I know," she quipped. "You never sleep. Hardly ever."

Through the evening Daria wished her mother had gone out with one of her friends from the bank. Peg yawned and kept saying how tired she was after entertaining Don and Carola; still, she stayed in front of the TV set.

All through the evening Carola's words and their many meanings kept singing through Daria's head. She remembered every word with astonishing clarity. She had told her mother at supper about having gone out with Aunt Carola.

Peg had only looked up briefly from her food and murmured, "Oh, that's nice." Then she had turned the conversation to mundane things. Sitting opposite her, Daria had felt stifled, but she had fought down anger, surprised that it was possible.

"Did Carola come here again this morning?" Peg asked, finally. "Is that why you cleaned the house?"

"No," Daria said. "I did that afterward."

"Why?" Her mother continued to look down at her food. Then slowly she raised her eyes to meet Daria's, repeating, "Why?"

"I—I did it," Daria said slowly, "for you."

"Thank you, Daria." Peg's smile was gentle. "It makes me very glad when you do that for me."

They spoke no more for a time, but it was a good, warm silence.

"When you were little," Peg murmured, chuckling, "remember how you used to make me breakfast on Sundays?"

Daria nodded, smiling slightly. "Orange juice, tea and toast. I usually burned the toast."

"I didn't care. You used to walk in with that big tray . . ."

They sat together watching TV in the living room, Daria thinking of the many things Carola had said, fitting them all together now, beginning to understand things about herself and her mother, seeing it anew.

At last Daria stood up from watching TV. She stretched and said, "I guess I'll go to bed. I'm tired, too."

Inside she felt the first faint tingling of excitement that was very like a small child's thrill at a birthday party or a first trip to Disneyland. Tonight! Tonight! Surely after such a day there would be something special for tonight. And she herself would bring it into being. She would call. The call would be answered. But how? Now, confronted with the task, she asked herself, How does one summon a spirit?

"Mom," Daria said suddenly. "Would you let me borrow just a little of that perfume I gave you?"

Her mother hesitated, then sighed and made her voice light. "Sure. Help yourself."

Later, Daria poured several drops of the perfume into her bathwater. She lay back, surrounded by the warmth and the fragrance, and gazed down through half-closed eyes at her legs, her arms, her middle. She was too pale. She ought to lie in the sun and get a good tan, like Kelly.

Kelly . . . last summer they'd done everything together. They'd talked about how this summer they would go up to Paradise Lake where Kelly's parents were renting a cabin. All winter and spring she and Kelly had talked about it.

Daria closed her eyes, moving her shoulders to let the water lap up over her back, relaxing.

As she thought about Kelly now, it was without resentment. For three years they'd done everything together. They had giggled at the same jokes, gossiped about the same people, grew from talking about swimming and bicycling to wondering which boys they'd like and what sort of bikinis they would buy. Nobody had ever made Daria feel quite the way Kelly did. With Kelly, everything had been double the fun, because Kelly could see the humorous side of nearly every situation. It didn't matter that she got mad sometimes, because she never held a grudge.

But now, as she thought about it, Daria could see that they might have drifted apart before too long. Maybe the incident with the dish had just brought it all to a climax. Even back last summer, while she liked Kelly as much as ever, little things were beginning to bother her. Like the way Kelly kept wanting to do the same thing over and over again, instead of trying something new. It was Kelly who always wanted to go back to the roller coaster, just as she wanted to see the same movie six times over and play

144

endless games of Monopoly, as they'd been doing since they were ten.

Daria lay down deep in the tub, in the warm, soothing water. Next year, she thought, they'd all be going to Marble Beach High. They'd have lots of friends. Maybe Kelly would be one of them. She hoped so; she missed Kelly. But she'd never be the only one again. Daria sighed softly, but without sorrow. It was all right. They were past the stage of "best friends." They were all changing.

But it would have been nice, Daria thought wistfully, for her and Kelly to have shared all this. It was too bad that Kelly would never know about the kinds of things Daria was experiencing. Kelly could have understood some of it, she was sure.

She realized she'd been whispering to herself. No other sounds, not even the radio music, came from Peg's room. She was surely asleep. It was past midnight. Even Priscilla was bedded down in her basket, sound asleep. Outside the moon was full. Its light shone against the textured glass of the bathroom window, forming curiously changing patterns of dots and squares.

Daria turned on the hot water faucet with her foot, just enough to let the water retain its warmth. Suddenly the light in the bathroom went out.

Instinctively Daria stood up in the tub, reaching for her towel. Then she sat down again to let the warm water surround her. With a calm and complete certainty, she knew that the moment was right.

She whispered, "Grandma? Is it you?"

"Yes." A whisper returned to her, rustling through the very walls, curling in around the edges of the window.

Daria turned, staring at the window with its wavering, winking lights. "Where are you?"

"Look over here."

Poised over the toilet seat, standing not upon it but several inches above it, was the figure, looking very much like white cheesecloth a trifle damp and blowing on a clothesline.

"Why are you standing there?" Daria inquired softly. "And why did you come now? I was going to get dressed and . . ."

"Modesty!" She chuckled. "It's not as though we weren't related, child. Do you really think clothes make a difference to me, in my condition?" She laughed so heartily that her shape wavered and shook, and Daria put her finger to her lips.

"Shh! You'll wake my mother, and she'll think I'm. . . ."

"Bombed?" She cried gleefully. "Off your rocker?" She laughed again, obviously proud of her slang. "She can't hear me. Only you. Peggy is not—poor girl—very flexible."

"But I didn't call you," Daria said. "I was planning to call you after I got out of the tub."

"Maybe you didn't realize it," She said, "but you did summon me. Not with your voice, but with your mind. Words are not really so important after all, are they? A wise old soul once told me, 'We know those things best that we know without words.' And some things—like feelings—are often best expressed without words."

"Like a painting," Daria mused. "Like love."

"You reached me without words," She continued, "with your mind. That, my dear, is how I managed to contact you to begin with. If your mind had been tight and sealed, it would have been impossible. You gave me a chance . . . it's difficult to explain. Do you understand?"

"A little," Daria said. Rob must have been right about being relaxed. "What shall I call you?" she asked.

"Grandma is a good name." She quivered and seemed

146

to be almost breaking in several places, like ripples on a lake.

"Are you coming apart?" Daria cried, aghast.

Laughter caused the shape to shift again. "What you see," She replied, "is the best I can do. I must confess I'm really not very good at this."

"Is that why the other afternoon you were so faint?"

"Was I?" It seemed to amuse Her. "I thought I was doing rather well, especially considering it was daylight. But now you see the proof of what I've been trying to explain to you; spirits—as you would call me—are not infallible. We are still learning, too. Of course, I've had a head start. But, enough of this. I haven't much time . . ."

"Why not?"

"Energy, child. This is costing me a great deal of energy."

"Grandma!" Daria sat upright. "Tell me, why do you come?"

"To teach you, my dear, about that other side of your nature. To help you be aware. . . . You have talked to Carola," She stated.

"Yes. I think—it seems impossible, I know, but I think I can remember back to when I was a baby in Missouri and leaving you."

"It is not impossible," She said gently. "Part of you remembers all things. Most people are afraid to remember. It was sad."

"Yes. I remember being sad," Daria said, "and I remember the smell of your perfume."

"Feelings are not forgotten," She said. "I missed you, too," She said, but without regret. "Life is the way it is."

"Why did she take me away?" Daria half rose out of the tub, and as she did so, the apparition receded. Back

147

under the water again, Daria turned on the hot faucet with her toe, asking politely, "Does water bother you?"

"Not at all. Your mother took you away because she did not want me to influence you. Peggy didn't approve of my—my career. When I predicted that poor Tracy would meet his death, and then it did happen, Peg was terrified and angry. I believe she thought that somehow I *caused* his death."

"That's absurd!" Daria exclaimed. "You wouldn't! To know something is not to *cause* it."

"She thought my mediumship and everything connected with it would . . . how did she put it? She said she didn't want her baby infected by trash and evil nonsense. So she left, and I never heard from her again."

"I missed you so," Daria murmured.

"That's water under the bridge now," She said briskly. "What I want to know is, how are you going to grow from now on?"

"What do you mean? How can I answer?" Daria felt suddenly very aware of her nudity, and the water was getting cold.

"Peggy came to hate me," She said, and Her voice wavered, as if the distance between them were growing. "She also came to hate all things of the spirit, all having to do with that soft, inner voice. Because that's the part of us that can be hurt the hardest. Do you understand?" The voice grew faint.

"I want to understand!" Daria cried. "If I call, will you come again?"

"I'll try," She said. "I, too, am limited. The crab, whose life is lived in two dimensions, must think the birds are gods."

"Grandma, I'm going to . . ."

In that moment She vanished. Simultaneously the light

winked once, as if the bulb had been loose. Then it shone again steadily.

Quickly Daria got out of the tub, dried herself and hurried to call Rob, to tell him her summons had been answered.

"It's a once in a lifetime chance," Daria told her mother, "to work with an artist like Miss Morehead. I'm not going to miss that." After the third day of summer school, Daria had decided to drop the other two courses and concentrate on art.

"If you learned to type," Peg said sullenly, "you could probably get a job next summer. Sometimes they hire part-time typists at the bank. You're getting older. You can't just play around all the time."

Daria said nothing, but the familiar heaviness settled inside her. She wondered—does everyone feel that they don't really fit into their own family? Surely her mother had felt that way. It was strange to think of Peg at thirteen, having to fight for an ordinary and proper life the way she, Daria, had to fight for the right to dream and to paint.

The art teacher, Antoinette Morehead, was a tough, frosty woman in her sixties. In the first week of class she dismissed eight students for "lack of aptitude," and several more because they hadn't "cultivated the proper attitude toward art."

Those remaining, she regarded as her children, to be pampered and prodded, bullied and coaxed. "Come, now, my dears, look how the sun strikes that windowpane! Show me, show me what you really see. Paint that beam of light. White? Silver? Ah, nonsense, there are four hundred shades of white, and more. Speak to me! Speak to me in color!"

And Daria would smile to herself as she worked, fulfilled at last, listening to someone she could really understand, just as she could understand the Grandma.

When it came to art, Miss Morehead could be ferociously sarcastic. "Are you afraid to reveal yourselves? What's this—is your emotion so rare that we can't share it? Come now, surely you don't see the world the same way I do—I'm an old frump! Oh, you want to mimic me? There is no room among artists for imitators—go to the zoo and speak to the parrots, but get out of my class if you only want to copy!"

All morning she badgered and coaxed. She drilled them in techniques, introduced them to works of great artists, told them to find "the color of the inner eye," as she called it, and each day she crooned to them, "Make this your summer of art. This summer, my children, there need be no time for anything in your lives except art."

When an assignment or "a study" was completed and brought to her, Antoinette Morehead had a way of simply raising her eyebrows and murmuring, "And now? Now, again."

Then the student would know that there were countless alternative ways to do the thing better, to do it again and again, until painting and sketching consumed nearly the entire day and often half the night.

Peg fussed and fretted, or she remained tight-lipped and silent. If Daria devoted herself to painting, Peg muttered, "You'll make yourself sick."

If Daria took time off to go to the beach with Rob and Nan, Peg made a grimace. "You're turning into a regular beach bum, Daria. Next you'll get sunstroke."

What does she want? Daria asked herself, seething inside. What does she want of me? Why couldn't her mother be more like her grandmother, or even like Antoinette Morehead? Yes, yes, Daria thought, she should have been her grandmother's child. And then she realized that in a way, she was. She *was* the child of Rose Whittlesey, as much as she was the child of Peg Peterson.

Daria caught her breath sharply. Yes, this was the very thing her mother had feared most. That the child would become like the grandmother. That Daria would be catapulted into a world which, to Peg, seemed monstrous and unnatural, where there was only danger, death and sorrow. For Peg could not distinguish between *knowing* and *causing*. Peg simply was not ready for matters of the spirit. Perhaps she never would be.

As Daria stood outside the apartment where she had been watching the sunset, learning its colors, she knew her mother's fears. She knew, for as Priscilla left her side and moved toward a nearby oak tree, Daria remembered a day when she was only eight. Priscilla was still a kitten, but nearly full grown. They had lived in another place then, with a childless woman next door who spent her time gardening. The woman was outside watering when Daria began to scream.

"Child, what is it? Can I help?" The woman hurried over to find Daria in tears, straining to reach Priscilla who was scrambling faster and faster up a tall pine tree.

"My kitty! My kitty is going too high!" Daria had cried, terrified that the cat would fall and be killed.

"No, no," the woman soothed her. "It's not too high for a kitty at all. Your kitty must do this. It is in her nature to climb trees. You must understand, what would be dangerous for you is exactly right for her."

"But why?" Daria had cried. "I want her to stay down here with me! I'm scared."

"She cannot stay with you all the time, child. Your being afraid changes nothing. Watch how much fun she has up there! Let her be. Let her be a cat."

Now Daria sat down on the steps, watching Priscilla as she lay on a stout limb in the oak, looking down. "Hello, cat!'' she said softly, smiling to herself. Perhaps someday her mother would look at her this way, without fear, without needing to change her.

"It's not her fault, you see," Daria murmured to Priscilla, for the cat had scampered down and now moved into Daria's lap. "It's very hard for her, Priss, because she's so scared—scared for me. I guess she doesn't mean to be so tough and stern. It's just her way. Of course, we would rather see her smile more often . . ."

Yes, that was what was missing in more ways than one. Perhaps she would learn ways to help bring that smile, even that wispy suggestion of a smile, back to her mother's lips. It was this softness, she saw now, that was missing from the sketch she was doing of her.

From memory, because Peg would never pose, Daria had begun to sketch her mother's face, but it was always wrong. It was too hard, too fierce, too unyielding. She had wanted to use that face in conjunction with another, older, face, using color and form in a way she had never done before.

When she recognized her problem, she began again. She sketched for hours, changing her drawing, improving it, looking forward to the day when she would get it right and do it, finally, in oils.

One afternoon, when Daria had not been thinking about art at all, everything suddenly came together. She and Rob had met at the mini-park. Daria had been watching the ducks as they swam round and round, until she realized that for some time she had been in a state of suspension, neither daydreaming nor sleeping, but some nearly trance-like state in between.

She stood up suddenly. "Rob, I've got to go home."

"Is something wrong?" He stood up, too, frowning.

"No. Something's finally right! I've got to go home and paint."

He nodded and walked back to the apartment with her. She went straight to her room and set up the easel. Immediately she was caught up in that other world—that secret place that had always, always existed within her, but that she had only recently learned to define—the other world of her painting. Usually, several minutes would pass while she made the transition between the hectic, outside world and the other, inner place from which she could create. Now it happened immediately.

In her mind, the painting was already complete. She had only to let it happen. She had only to let go of thoughts and doubts, let her mind float free, as she had done in summoning the vision. She had only to relax and reach far, far inside herself, and then to let herself paint.

Dimly she heard Peg unlock the front door. Later, when her mother called her for supper, Daria called back.

"Don't make me eat now, Mom! I'm busy."

"But you have to eat, Daria!"

"I already had a sandwich and some fruit."

It wasn't true, but that didn't matter. Nothing mattered now except that feeling, that letting go of something but grasping something even more important, more important than any talk, clearer than any words, and she thought joyously, *oh, yes, we know those things best that we know without words*.

16

*

Since Carola's visit and Daria's vision in the bathtub, she and Nan had become even closer.

"You have something very special," Nan had murmured when Daria had gone into details about what the Grandmother had said. "I—I feel proud to know you. Sometimes, too," she admitted, "I'm jealous."

"Don't be," Daria said gently. "It's a mixed blessing—being so different."

"No, it's not," Nan said. "I feel as if you've got a head start on everyone else."

"Sometimes I still doubt it's really happened, you know? I'm never sure She'll come again . . ."

"Maybe if you believed in Her more—and in your own power. You're always questioning it."

Daria nodded. "I can't just accept things without asking questions. It wouldn't be logical. Some people go too far, believing everything without even thinking."

"How do you ever know when you can trust your visions, then?" Nan asked.

"I guess it'll take experience," Daria replied.

"Like riding a bike?" Nan laughed.

"Yeah. I guess so. Like my dream. I had it again last night—about the car crash. But it was different, and somehow I'm sure I won't ever have it again. There was the train and the crash, and my mother slumped over the wheel. But it went on from there. I saw myself getting out of the other car, going to her. I opened the door of her car and pulled her out. She'd cut her face, but she was all right. In the dream I took her to a small diner and got her a cup of coffee. Then we sat there talking and she—that was the odd thing—she called me 'Mother'.''

They were both silent for several minutes.

"Mother," Nan repeated softly. "That means you had changed roles, in a way. You were the one in charge."

"Maybe it's not so much a matter of being *in charge*," Daria said slowly, "but being the one to reach out. Maybe I can handle some things that my mother can't."

"Like the visions," Nan said soberly. "Like having ESP."

"So I've got to handle this part of it, and just let her . . ."

"Let her sit back and—and let you take charge. Because this whole thing," Nan said, speaking rapidly now, excitedly, "this whole psychic thing upsets her so much. See, the car crash must just have been a symbol for all the problems you've been having—like the clashing of *ideas* between you and your mother. In the dream, she's the one who gets hurt by the confrontation. You don't. You go to help her . . ."

Daria nodded. "I've known from the start that I'd be on my own in this," she said soberly. Then she gave Nan a quick smile. "Except for you and Rob," she added.

"So your dream wasn't a premonition at all," Nan said.

"I'm relieved about that," Daria said. "But I'm going to have to learn how to interpret my dreams, and to figure out how to tell the difference between real premonitions and phoney ones, and those that are symbolic. How do you learn things like that?"

Nan shook her head. "Maybe every—every psychic has to find his own way. Maybe She will help you. Or maybe it would help to work with Rob's dad."

"Only problem is, I'd need my mother's permission, and I'm not willing to tell her about these—these . . ."

"Honestly, Daria," Nan exclaimed, her expression of amazement and disbelief, "don't you think she knows?"

"But how could she know?"

"I think a mother would just know."

For days Daria pondered that thought, and as she confronted it squarely, she became certain that Nan was right. Of course Peg knew. Perhaps she did not know precisely what was happening, but she surely knew that Daria was different. One night she, Daria, had fallen asleep in the old rocker, the sketch pad on her lap. She had awakened suddenly with a start, to see the sketch pad on the floor and her mother standing across the room, about to go out the door.

She had stared for a moment at her mother's back, knowing that a moment earlier her mother had stood beside the rocking chair looking down, staring down at the sketch of her own mother, Rose Whittlesey.

"Mom?" Daria had called into the stillness. "I—I guess I'll get undressed and go to bed."

"Hurry," came Peg's voice, muffled and noncommital. "It's getting late."

The painting was finished at last. She had done it in oils, in a watery, almost eerie blending of colors, completely unlike anything she had ever seen before.

She brought the painting to school the next day, before it was even quite dry to the touch. As usual, she simply stood it up on one of the easels beside the teacher's worktable, and waited. She tried to make herself concentrate on the study for the day, but she kept wondering, in agony, when or whether the teacher would make comment. Suppose she delivered one of her stinging, sarcastic criticisms? Daria didn't think she could bear it.

156

"Daria Peterson!" That low, frosty voice broke through the murmur of students working on their assignments. "Daria Peterson has done something quite new," she said. In the teacher's eyes was a glint Daria had not seen before. "This is a finished work, students. This is art."

Her eyes sought Daria, and the gaze seemed to pierce right through her, stronger, more resolute than words, and more filled with meaning. Almost sternly she said, "Daria Peterson, it isn't going to be easy. Don't ever think it will. But paint. Just paint."

From her place at the table, Daria nodded, her heart too full to speak.

That night she took her painting back home and placed it in her closet, the picture turned toward the wall. Several nights later, Daria discovered it had been moved. She knew, because her old roller skates now stood neatly beside the painting. Her mother had seen, and still she was silent.

Lying in bed, feeling the cool sheets against her legs, Daria sighed. It was a silence of Peg's own choosing. She, Daria, could not break it. She must simply accept it.

Gently she fell asleep, only to wake up almost immediately, hearing Priscilla's light scratching at the door.

Quickly Daria let the cat in and onto her bed. She lay stroking the soft fur while Priscilla purred and showed the tip of her tiny pink tongue, and with a flood of well-being and utter calm, Daria knew this was the time.

"Grandma!" Her whisper was gentle, but firm. "Grandma!"

When She appeared, Priscilla opened her eyes wide, blinked, then put her head down between her paws, purring peacefully.

"Your cat knows me now," She said. "That is good. And you," She continued, "are seeing many new things."

"Yes," Daria said. "I have finally finished a painting

157

that is complete. My teacher likes it. Is that why you came to begin with? To help me with my art?''

Her form seemed to sparkle. ''I never told you to take art in summer school! No, it wasn't that. But, of course, all things are related. To unfold in one area brings unfolding in another.''

''Unfold,'' Daria mused. ''I like that word. It is like a flower.''

''An unfolding of the *mind*,'' She said.

''You told me at the start,'' Daria said, ''that I'm more than just a body. I still have so many doubts,'' she admitted.

''That's good,'' She said. ''One must first doubt, in order to seek and discover. You are learning.''

''What must I learn? Can you teach me?''

''You know,'' She said, and Priscilla purred loudly in her sleep.

''It's more than art,'' Daria stated. ''It's everything . . .''

''Take care of her!'' She said with a sudden urgency. ''Keep her from being too lonely. Give her . . .''

In that instant the form vanished, and Daria's door was flung open. Peg stood there, pale and tense in the meager light from the window. Without turning on the light, she spoke.

''I know you're awake, Daria. And I know you've got that cat in here with you.''

''All right,'' Daria said wearily. ''So, I'll put the cat out.''

''Daria!'' It was a cry. ''I don't care about the cat! I want you to know, Daria, that I know exactly what you're doing.''

''What are you talking about?'' Daria's voice rose. ''What do you mean? I'm not doing anything!''

''I know exactly. Because I have lived it all. All of it, and I tell you, it's a terrible thing. It eats away at you,

158

little by little. Pretty soon you don't even know who you are, and you're so ashamed . . ."

Daria jumped out of bed, snapped on her light and stood before her mother.

"Mom! I know who I am. Mom, look at me."

For a long moment Peg looked at her, as if seeing her closely for the first time in months. In the mirror Daria could see both her own reflection and her mother's, and beyond these, in the eye of her mind, she could see Rose Whittlesey, and she knew that something unmistakable in her own features showed their bond. As if Peg had voiced it, Daria could read the thought, *My God, the child even looks like her! There, about the eyes and the chin. Even the sweep of her eyelashes. Why haven't I seen it before?*

Softly Daria said, half smiling, "Mom, don't worry about me. I'm really OK."

Peg nodded, with a certain sense of finality, and said, "I just want you to realize that I cannot be responsible." Then, turning, she added, "You are staying up much too late these nights."

For a time Daria slept. When she awakened, it seemed to be near dawn. Daria could tell it was near daybreak, just as she knew, even before she opened her eyes, that She was there again—or perhaps She had never left during that interlude.

"Does she know about me and you, Grandma?" Daria whispered.

"There are different levels of knowing," She replied.

"I'm sure she saw the painting," Daria said. "She must know that you and I communicate. Why won't she admit it? I should think she'd be curious . . ."

"Curiosity," said She, quivering so that silvery particles shimmered, "curiosity involves risk. And my Peggy won't take any risks. Not after that large risk that turned out so badly. Even as a child, you know, she always wanted to play it safe, and as you say—straight.''

"She's still afraid of anything she can't see or touch."

"Terribly afraid! She fears losing control over her life."

"The way I did," Daria murmured. "I thought that, but it isn't really true."

She said, "Truth is the hardest thing to discover. Sometimes it's not comfortable."

In a low voice Daria said, "It hurt me when I learned about my father."

"I know."

"That was the truth," Daria said. "But why did I need to know it? Maybe it's better not to know some things."

"Maybe," She agreed.

"But it was the beginning," Daria said. "If I hadn't found out about my father . . .''

"It was a new truth for you," She explained. "You needed to accept it before you were ready to seek other truths. You had to be told something that could be proven. To open your mind, you see, to still other truths."

"Do you know them all?"

She laughed, a tinkling sound. "Far, far from it, my dear. It's a question of opening doors and more doors."

She seemed to move closer, yet there had been no real motion. "I wanted you to understand this," She said, "and to help me. Take care of her. She needs you."

"To do what? How can I?"

"You know," She murmured. "I wanted to give her love." The shape seemed to glow even more brightly, as if a white flame had been kindled. "I was not able. From me, she would not accept it. So give her love. For both of us."

Summer school was nearly over. Rob, Nan and Daria talked about how they'd spend the rest of summer, wishing they were older, wishing they could drive to the lake. "Oh, you can tell your dad," Daria said, "that he's got himself a new subject."

"Really!" Rob was beaming. "Hey, that's great! But how did you ever get your mother to . . ."

Daria shrugged. Somehow, she didn't want to share this, even with Rob and Nan. It didn't seem fair. She had asked her mother last night, but only once, but perhaps something in the set of her jaw or the look in her eyes had made Peg catch her breath.

"You want to do some work with Rob's dad? With a psychologist?"

"Yes, Mother. He wants me to do some tests, to find out how my ability . . ."

Peg held up her hand, forestalling explanation. "Now, Daria, if you and that man want to waste your time on such nonsense, what do I care? So, go sit there in a drab office and waste away your summer. Just don't complain to me later that you didn't have enough time at the beach."

"You'll have to sign this note," Daria said, holding it out.

"Very well. Now, will you please finish the dishes."

Daria had turned to the sink, careful to avoid meeting her mother's gaze. Peg had, Daria knew, given all she could, done all that she dared.

Now Daria told Rob, "Just call and let me know when your dad wants me to start. It ought to be interesting."

"You guys want to go to Polo Joe's?"

"I'd better get home," Daria said. "My last project is due Friday."

"We'll walk you," Nan and Rob said.

They began the climb up the hill, Nan and Rob laughing and talking about something that Daria couldn't quite hear. Or if she heard, she couldn't absorb, for a strange tingling sensation began in her fingers and toes, and a sudden breathlessness made her gasp.

"Dari, something wrong?"

"No. No, I'm OK."

They continued, Rob and Nan walking slightly behind Daria, while resolutely Daria proceeded, feeling so very odd, just as she'd felt the night of the carnival. She shrugged it off, reached her apartment house, took the key from her pocket, put the key into the lock—and suddenly it all stood out before her, clear.

"Kelly!" She screamed so violently that Nan and Rob stopped, frozen, trembling at the sound of it. "Kelly! Oh, my God."

Now, no thought intruded, only a mighty surge of energy propelled her, pushed her down, down the hill, with Rob and Nan dazedly following, shouting down, "Dari! Daria, what's wrong? Daria, wait for us!"

Down, down the hill so fast that there seemed to be no breath in her body, and the hot pavement seemed to thrust itself up against her feet as she ran toward her destination, toward Carni Square and the Ferris wheel, the Ferris wheel where Kelly Baxter and Charlie Lacey stood hand in hand, waiting while the other kids climbed up into the baskets, moving in couples or sometimes three in a seat, the bar being locked into place, then the man turning the handle of the little wheel to bring another basket down for the next pair to enter . . .

"Kelly!" Daria screamed, the blood pounding in her ears, screaming out with her entire being, although she was still over a block away. "Kelly! Don't go on it! Kelly!"

Kelly and Charlie Lacey, holding hands, looked at each other smiling, because they would sit very close in the small basket on the Ferris wheel, and they loved whirling round and round, faster and faster.

The man began to grumble, "Hurry up, you kids, can't wait all day," as he turned the wheel once again, stepped aside and waited for Kelly and Charlie to enter . . .

Down the street, her throat dry, lungs aching, Rob and Nan fast behind, Daria came racing into view of the Ferris wheel, screaming with a last mighty effort, "Kelly! Kelly, don't go on it!"

In that moment the man gave the handle a crank. He grumbled angrily, "Can't wait all day. Can't you kids ever make up your minds?" for Kelly and Charlie had turned and stepped aside at the frantic, insane screaming, and even as Daria stood, gasping and wild-eyed, the Ferris wheel gained momentum until it whirled above them in a flying arc, faster and faster, its motion tied grotesquely to the screams of the people in the baskets, the screams and laughter mingling with that one impossible, unexplainable thing that all parents always fear whenever their children go on rides. It happened.

The one basket remaining empty, the basket that was meant for Kelly Baxter and Charlie Lacey—spun off. It twisted with a cracking, grinding noise, and it came crashing to the ground.

Everything stopped. Time, it seemed, stopped while people gathered together the meaning of it, the horror of it, and the mercy. The miracle.

For a moment Kelly and Daria clutched at each other. Then they drew apart, Kelly taking Charlie Lacey's hand, Daria standing close to Rob and Nan, while all the other people looked on, numb and silent in that moment before the shouting and the talk would begin.

Daria and Kelly only looked at each other, and now both of them knew. Without ever any explanation, they both knew that a door had been opened, and that beyond, another door was waiting.